The Road
&
Other Tales of Intrigue

Written by Colin Fantham

Copyright protected © All rights reserved
No AI was used in the making of this book

ISBN: 978-1-918038-94-1

Contents

1	The Road to Fear	3
2	Spencer Tate's Dream	16
3	A Curious Reunion	24
4	A Chance Encounter	35
5	Murder in Act Two	44
6	The Suitcase	64
7	The Bookworm and The Ghosts	76
8	Eleanor Finally Meets Her Match	89
9	A Flicker of Light in the Shadows	101
10	A Student of Death	116
11	The Many Lives of Henry	127
12	The Man Who Made Them Laugh	142
13	The Doppelganger	153

The Road to Fear

The snow began to fall more frequently as they continued to drive, frantically, late into the night. Visibility of the road ahead was fast diminishing with each passing minute and the young married couple had driven for what seemed like hours in their old black saloon car.

They were hopelessly lost.

Ben felt a growing sense of unease, and gripped the steering wheel tight in frustration.

'This is ridiculous,' he muttered under his breath, and craned his neck forward as though he would be able to see better through the worsening weather. 'Bloody satnav's as useful as a chocolate teapot,' he said, and stroked the dark stubble on his chin, which he often did when stressed.

Jennifer checked her mobile phone. 'There's still no signal,' she said, a hint of panic now distinctly etched in her voice. She wiped the sweat from her brow, and pushed her long auburn hair back from her eyes. 'Where *are* we?'

'Hard to say... I haven't seen a road sign for miles.

Jennifer felt her swollen stomach. 'That's comforting,' she said, facetiously.

Ben glanced nervously at his wife.

'Bad?'

'The contractions are getting more frequent. The sooner we find that hospital the better,' she said.

'Keep breathing deep gulps of air. Remember what the doctor said.'

Jennifer tried to remain calm but the situation they were in was now dire. 'We should have called for an ambulance.'

Ben felt the burden of guilt tear into him; after all, it was *his* idea to drive them to the hospital when Jennifer's waters broke; now he thought about it, it was also *his* idea for them to up sticks and move from London to a remote rented cottage in North Wales, where he worked from home as a consultant in IT.

'I'm sure we'll find that hospital before long,' he said, doubting his own words.

As they continued on their interminable journey, the road began to narrow, and they found themselves driving aimlessly through a tree-lined track.

'Toto, I don't think we're in Kansas anymore,' said Ben, trying to make light of the situation but desperately looking at his new surroundings, feeling a growing sense of alarm inside.

Jennifer was now at her wits end. 'That's not funny!' she snapped.

Ben felt his cheeks flush.

'The road's too narrow to turn back. I'm sure this has to lead to somewhere,' he said, his voice now betraying a modicum of panic.

Jennifer looked out of the window as the branches of the snow-covered trees began brushing the side of the car. 'I'm not sure I share your confidence, Ben,' she said, solemnly.

Their journey continued in an eerie silence inside the car as the elements continued to deteriorate.

They both saw the white-haired old man suddenly step out in front of them, waving his hands wildly, but it was too late to avoid impact. Ben instinctively turned the steering wheel sharply to the right.

The car slammed into a tree.

Ben was the first to come to his senses. He couldn't tell how long he had passed out for, but as his surroundings slowly came into focus, he realised with alarm that Jennifer was sitting still, as though sleeping, beside him. The deflated airbags hung lifeless before them. He hurriedly unbuckled his seat belt, reached out, and gently shook Jennifer's shoulder.

'Jenny... *Jenny.*'

Gradually, Jennifer stirred from her concussion and faced Ben. 'Wh... What happened?' she asked, sluggishly.

'The old man,' he said. 'He came out of nowhere.'

Jennifer thought long and hard.

'I remember now,' she said. 'Oh god,' she exclaimed. 'I think we hit him.'

Ben opened his door and ventured out into the dark snow-laden wilderness. 'I'll see if I can find him,' he called back. 'He can't be far.' He closed the door behind him.

Ben stepped away from the car, his footsteps crunching in the deep snow about him. It was obvious that their vehicle was beyond repair - the front of it was completely crumpled and wedged into the trunk of a sturdy tree. Steam from the collapsed radiator plumed and evaporated into the cold night air. He searched around and well beyond the broken vehicle, in a desperate bid to find the stricken old man, but to no avail.

It was as if he had simply vanished.

In the distance, through a gap in the trees, Ben glimpsed a faint light. He returned to the car and sat beside Jennifer. 'He's not there,' he said, now shivering from cold. 'I looked all around.'

'Oh my god!' she yelled.

'He must have wondered off.'

They sat in silence as the gravity of their situation began to take hold.

Jennifer rubbed her stomach, protectively, and murmured in desperation: 'What are we going to do?' she cried.

'We can't stay here,' he said. 'The heater's packed up and the cold air is rapidly coming through the holes in the car.'

'What's the alternative?'

Ben reached over to the back seat and grabbed their coats. He passed Jennifer's coat to her, and began to put his own coat on.

'I saw a light in the distance. I'm pretty sure it was from a cottage. We'll have to make our way there. Do you think you can walk?'

Jennifer unbuckled her seat belt, and began putting on her coat. 'I can try,' she said, determinedly, her maternal instincts now taking control of her actions.

They exited the car, and stepped into the cold wilderness together.

Heading slowly for the dim light in the distance, Ben and Jennifer slowly, and carefully, traipsed through the crisp snowy landscape of trees and undulating terrain. Jennifer held on tightly to Ben's arm as the falling snow continued to hamper their progress.

'We'll be there soon enough,' said Ben, trying hard to sound as calm as he could, given their ominous circumstance. The image of the old man just before impact was firmly emblazoned on his mind; it was something that he would never be able to come to terms with, but he also knew that the survival of their first-born depended on them reaching sanctuary.

'My feet are so cold,' said Jennifer.

'Not long now. The light is a lot closer.'

The snowfall began to subside, and before long, as they continued on their hazardous journey, the stars were now sparkling brightly in the clear night sky. A shooting star glimmered briefly in the heavens above them but the aesthetic beauty of the moment was lost in their desperate struggle.

Ben and Jennifer ventured nearer to the light, like moths to a flame. A small cottage gradually came into view. It was an old building that had seen better days – dilapidated, aged, its façade covered in thick intrusive ivy. Smoke billowed from a tall intricate chimney. It was, nonetheless, a welcome sight to see, given their troubled situation.

They now stood before the front door, exhausted from their perilous trek through the snow.

Ben rapped on the door sharply with his knuckle. After a long silence the frail voice of an old woman was heard.

'Yes? Who's there?'

It was Ben who quickly responded first. 'We've been in an accident,' he said. 'Our car has broken down. Can we come in, please?'

'I don't see why you should,' replied the old woman, irritably. 'This is my home.'

'*Please!*' exclaimed Jennifer. 'I'm heavily pregnant.'

A lengthy contemplative silence ensued.

Several locks were heard being noisily unfastened. The door finally creaked open, revealing the old woman now standing before them; although diminutive in stature, she was an imposing figure with long black hair, dark eyes, and sharp facial features. She wore a long black dress that had seen better days.

The old woman looked first at Ben, with deep suspicion in her eyes, and then at Jennifer; she could tell from Jennifer's demeanour that she was telling the truth.

'You'd best come in,' she said, begrudgingly, and stood aside to let them in. 'I had a feeling that somebody would turn up this evening,' she said, mysteriously.

As the door was closed behind them, Ben and Jennifer found themselves standing in a small dark dining room that belonged to an earlier era. Wood crackled noisily within an old stone fireplace, and the smell of smoke pervaded the atmosphere around them. The room was thankfully very warm and was lit by an abundance of candles. A tall shelving unit full of aged, well-read, books stood adjacent to a small window. At the far end of the room was an old wooden staircase. Around the perimeter of the room was a couple of battered armchairs and a small sofa, upon which lay a black cat sleeping blissfully. A small square wooden table, with two chairs, was in the middle of the room; upon the table was a ceramic tea jar and two porcelain dinner plates and matching teacups with saucers, as though an expectant visitor was awaited.

'Let me take your coats.'

Ben and Jennifer took off their coats and passed them to her.

'Thank you so much. We're so sorry to intrude,' said Ben, rubbing his hands for warmth.

'We were desperate,' said Jennifer.

'Do you have a phone?' asked Ben.

'Oh no,' said the old woman, with some disdain. 'I've never felt the need for one of *those*,' she said, dismissively. 'I'll put these in the other room.' She opened a nearby door, and left the room.

Ben and Jennifer looked around the room.

'It's like we time-travelled to the nineteen-thirties,' whispered Ben; he picked up one of the old books from a shelf, and read its title: 'Herbal Remedies for all Ailments.'

'Perhaps she's a witch?' suggested Jennifer, discreetly.

'She said she had a feeling about us turning up on her doorstep. You could be right.'

'It *is* quite spooky in here, isn't it?' she surmised, looking slowly around the room.

Ben saw a framed photograph next to one of the books on a shelf; he replaced the book, picked up the photograph, and carefully scrutinised it; it was of a white-haired old man, sitting in an armchair, who looked terrifyingly familiar.

'Oh my god,' he exclaimed, under his breath.

'What is it?'

Ben showed the photograph to Jennifer.

'It's *him*,' he declared.

'Are you sure?'

'His image is vividly imprinted upon my brain. It's him alright.'

The old woman re-entered the room. Ben quickly returned the photograph to the shelf. The sense of guilt he felt enveloped him.

'I see you've met my husband,' said the old woman.

Ben was taken aback. 'Your… husband?' he blurted out.

'We've been married for over fifty years.'

Ben and Jennifer looked to each other in shock; their eyes betrayed the realisation of the predicament they now found themselves in.

'I'll make you some hot chocolate. You look as though you've seen a ghost.'

An awkward silence was punctured by Jennifer. 'That's very kind of you,'

she said, coyly, and winced suddenly as she experienced a particularly painful contraction.

'Do sit down,' said the old woman to Jennifer. 'Take the weight off your feet.'

'Thank you.'

Jennifer gratefully sat on the sofa next to the sleeping cat.

'We're *so* sorry to inconvenience you,' said Ben.

'I don't normally have visitors. My son will be over early in the morning,' she said. 'He likes to keep an eye on me.

Thinks I'm losing my marbles.' She looked to her black cat, who was still fast asleep. 'Griselda,' she called.

The cat awoke from its slumber, stretched, and obediently jumped from the sofa, and stood beside the old woman's feet, pressing itself affectionately against her ankles.

The old woman went into her kitchen, closely followed by Griselda, and closed the door behind her.

Ben sat next to his wife on the sofa. They felt as though their world had collapsed around them. How were they going to tell the old woman that they had, in all likelihood, run over her husband? They sat in a long guilty silence, unable to come to terms with their situation.

It was Ben who was first to speak. 'We can't tell her,' he suggested. 'At least... not yet,' he said.

'What...? We *have* to, Ben,' she urged.

'We have enough to worry about. Besides... you've seen how old she looks. The shock might finish her off.'

'It was an accident. It wasn't our fault.'

'We'll tell her when the time is right,' said Ben, solemnly.

Jennifer nodded her reluctant agreement.

The old woman, closely followed by Griselda, returned to the room, bearing a small wooden tray with two steaming mugs of hot chocolate upon it. She set the tray down on the table, and then sat down in an armchair. The cat jumped up from the carpet onto the old woman's lap, and immediately began to sleep.

'Best let them cool down for a bit. They're very hot,' she said.

'You've been very kind,' said Jennifer.

'Have you lived here long?' asked Ben.

'It was my mother's cottage. I inherited it from her after she passed. When I married, it made sense for us to set up home here.'

'You must feel quite isolated?' said Ben.

The old woman thought for a long while. 'I have my books,' she said. 'And then there's the radio. I have Griselda, and of course I speak to my husband *all* the time.'

'You *do*?' asked Jennifer, timidly.

'Oh yes. It's a comfort. As I said, my son thinks I'm quite mad.'

Ben felt the agony of guilt eat into him and could contain himself no longer. 'I think there's something we need to tell you,' he said, tentatively.

'Oh god!' screamed Jennifer.

'It's okay, Jenny,' said Ben, reassuringly patting her knee. 'We can't keep-'

'No, you idiot! It's the *baby*. I think he's getting ready to make an appearance!' she shrieked, rubbing her stomach in earnest.

The old woman stood up quickly, spilling a shocked Griselda onto the floor in the process. 'Let me make up a bed for you. You'll be more comfortable there,' she said. She went to the staircase, closely followed by Griselda, and began slowly ascending the stairs.

'Are you okay, Jenny?' asked Ben.

'I think so,' she said, unconvincingly.

'We've got ourselves into a bit of a pickle, haven't we?'

Jennifer's breathing became erratic. 'That's the understatement of the century,' she gasped.

'Just think of the story we'll be able to tell the little one when he's older,' said Ben.

'That's not funny.'

'No,' said Ben, sheepishly, realising the seriousness of their situation. 'Of course not.'

After a while the old woman, followed by Griselda, returned to the dining room. 'I've prepared a room for you,' she said to Jennifer. 'I think you'll be more comfortable there. Do you think you will be able to manage the stairs? It's the first door on the left.'

'I can try,' said Jennifer.

'Let me help you,' said Ben, helping Jennifer to her feet.

Jennifer was less than impressed, and dismissed Ben's offer of assistance. 'I think you've done enough damage!' she snapped, and made her way to the staircase, slowly climbing the stairs in her own time.

The old woman called after her: 'I'll be up in a while to look in on you,' she said, reassuringly.

Griselda jumped onto the sofa, curled up, and began to sleep.

A door was soon heard opening and then closing.

Ben felt the full force of contrition engulf him. Not only had he and Jennifer, in all likelihood, run over the old woman's husband, but they were now imposing upon her goodwill. 'I'm sorry that things have turned out the way they have,' he said, emotionally, and sat back down on the sofa, beside Griselda.

The old woman passed a mug of hot chocolate to Ben. 'Life has a way of its own making. My husband told me as such earlier. You were not unexpected,' she said, cryptically. 'Do drink your hot chocolate; it has some special herbs in it which I prepared for you.'

Ben drank some of the hot chocolate; it tasted sweet and comforting. He felt the welcome liquid melt away some of the guilt and unease within him. 'Thank you,' he said, and downed the rest of the drink in one swallow.

The old woman stood before him. 'Don't worry about your wife,' she said, soothingly, and took the empty mug from Ben. 'I'll take good care of her.'

Ben began to feel overwhelmingly tired. The old woman standing in front of him began to look hazy. What did she mean, he wondered? His mind began to play tricks upon him. He suddenly thought of the old woman in a different light. Perhaps she wasn't the kindly Samaritan that they had thought she was. Perhaps she somehow now realised the fate of her husband. He looked at his surroundings: the candles; the books; the old woman's appearance; the black cat. Was this an eye for an eye? What did she put in his hot chocolate? Was Jennifer in danger? He tried to stay awake but he found himself drifting in a swirling sea that gradually consumed him.

Ben was now fast asleep…

He didn't know how long he had been asleep for, but the sound of the front door of the cottage opening and closing, and the morning light now streaming in from the small window, brought Ben gradually to his senses.

Standing before him was a man who looked as though he was in his late-fifties; he had short thinning black hair, wore an old tweed jacket and dark trousers, which were tucked into wellington boots, a wide paunch and a flushed face. He also had a shotgun in his hands that was pointed directly at Ben's head.

'Can I help you?' said the man; his warm Welsh accent betraying the underlying menace of his words.

Ben wondered if anything else could possibly go wrong. Events had conspired against them. If he hadn't been so bull-headed in the first place they wouldn't be in this mess. Ben stroked the dark stubble on his chin, in despair and contemplation; his thoughts were sharply interrupted by the old woman's voice from upstairs.

'Dafydd, is that you?' she called.

'Yes, Mam,' responded Dafydd. 'Is everything alright? You seem to have a visitor?'

The old woman slowly descended the stairs. When she reached the bottom of the stairs, and saw her son with his weapon pointed at Ben, she was horrified. 'Dafydd!' she cried. 'Put that thing away.'

'Are you sure? He looks a bit of a rogue to me,' said Dafydd, with conviction.

'Quite sure,' she said.

Dafydd reluctantly lowered his shotgun. 'Sorry about that,' he said to Ben. 'Can't be too careful, you see. There are a few bad apples in these parts.'

'Quite alright,' said Ben, unconvincingly.

Just then, Jennifer began descending the stairs; in her arms she carried a small bundle wrapped up in a shawl. 'Come and see your daughter,' she called to Ben, proudly.

Ben stood up and went to Jennifer. 'My... daughter?' He helped Jennifer to the sofa, and she gratefully sat down. The baby was making happy cooing and gurgling noises, and there was even a hint of a smile now and then. Ben picked up his newborn daughter and looked at her in wonder. The baby looked back at Ben and an instant indestructible bond was forged between them.

'Congratulations,' said Dafydd, warmly.

'Thank you,' said Ben, meekly. He felt overwhelmed.

'Mrs Marsden was so helpful,' said Jennifer, enthusiastically. 'She is a lifesaver. I couldn't have coped without her. She seemed to know exactly what to do.'

'Was that your car I saw on the way here?' asked Dafydd. 'It's in a pretty bad state. Written off, I'd say.'

'Afraid so,' said Ben, blissfully engaged with his daughter.

'I'll arrange for it to be towed away. Least I can do,' said Dafydd. Let me get you both to the hospital to be checked out.'

'Thank you,' said Jennifer. That's very kind of you.

Ben was in deep thought.

'Mrs Marsden…?' he enquired.

'Yes?'

'Your husband… you said you spoke to him and that we were expected.'

Dafydd gave a facial expression that suggested that his mother was not entirely of this world.

'Oh yes,' said Mrs Marsden. We talk to each other *all* the time. He told me to expect visitors, and he was right, wasn't he?'

'My father passed away five years ago,' said Dafydd, solemnly. 'His ashes are on the table.'

Ben and Jennifer looked to the table. Of course. The ceramic tea jar was an urn. All of a sudden it made perfect sense.

'We had such a bond between us,' said Mrs Marsden. 'Even after his death I can still hear his voice quite clearly.'

'He was a good man,' said Dafydd. 'Salt of the earth. He would give you the shirt off his back if you asked him. A pillar of the community, he was.'

Ben and Jennifer looked at each other. Their astonished look spoke a thousand words, and the relief that they now felt between them was palpable. If the old man hadn't appeared to them when he did then who knows what would have happened to them? They perhaps wouldn't have found sanctuary. Some things in life are beyond explaining.

'What is your first name, Mrs Marsden?' asked Jennifer.

'It's Mary. Why?'

Jennifer looked to Ben, and an unspoken agreement was made between them.

'We'd like to call our daughter Mary, after a very special lady,' she said. 'With your consent, of course,' she added.

'Why… that would be perfectly fine,' said Mrs Marsden, smiling broadly, and with that a tear slowly fell onto her cheek in her contentment.

Spencer Tate's Dream

Spencer Tate was in the middle of a recurring dream that he'd been having lately. It was dark and late into the night. He could see, quite clearly, tall imposing buildings of a certain age that he did not recognise but somehow, instinctively, he knew that he was walking through the streets of London. Occasionally he would see homeless people, young and old, sitting against walls or within the entrances of shops and offices, trying to protect themselves from the elements of the cold damp autumnal weather. Now and then he would see his reflection in the window of a building: a man in his thirties looking back at him, dressed in a shabby dark suit, white shirt and scuffed black shoes; his long blond hair and untidy beard betrayed a face that, although haunted by trepidation, still retained character and sensitivity.

He seemed to walk for miles, trying to find his way home, looking for a familiar landmark that would lead him to the comfort of his flat, but he never found one; instead, he kept on walking, aimlessly and hopelessly lost and all alone.

As the night wore on, a mist began to fall, as it usually did, and Spencer could now only see a few feet in front of him. A young man hurriedly ran past him, brushing his shoulder as he vanished into the mist; the sudden jolt made Spencer more wary of his surroundings. He realised that his suit was becoming damp from the mist that now enveloped him, and so he decided to seek shelter.

He came across an old bricked building which looked hundreds of years old; he noticed that the rickety wooden door had already been forced slightly ajar, so Spencer let himself in and closed the door behind him. Inside the building it was very dark and still, and the air had a musty aroma of age and decay. There was just enough light for him to see mannequins that were scattered here and there; their painted smiling faces above unadorned bodies made him shiver. It soon became apparent that the building was a department store from another era that had been left dilapidated, abandoned and unloved. He could just make out a staircase that led to another floor. He decided to explore his new surroundings.

As he was about to ascend the staircase, he suddenly heard an old man's echoey voice coming from somewhere behind him.

'You look lost.'

Spencer woke up with a start. A cold sweat beaded his forehead. Although he had become accustomed to some of the events in his recurring dream, nobody had ever spoken to him before. This was something new, and it was a shock. How was that possible? Dreams aren't supposed to work that way...

He thought about the dream while he was in the bathroom shaving, getting ready for work. That reflection in the window... that couldn't be him... could it? And that long hair... his was short and neat.

Sitting in the tube train travelling to work, Spencer let his mind wonder as he looked out to the darkness beyond the window; surely dreams are just dreams: figments of imagination brought about by events of the past? As a recently divorced father, he figured that the pressure of providing for his daughter, paying alimony and trying to keep his head above water was having a diverse effect on his mind. And then there was work... rumblings of redundancies loomed large. If he was laid off, how was he going to be able to cope? He was already behind in his rent, and the bills were stacking up. Normally he was optimistic but lately he found himself on the boundaries of despair.

Spencer worked for a banking customer service call-centre. Sitting at his workplace cubicle, he waited for the next irate customer to call; most of the calls were from disgruntled account holders who had managed to have their credit cards blocked through their own negligence. It was Spencer's job to resolve the issue. It was a soulless occupation that gave little or no job satisfaction, but he was grateful for the small income that he was paid for his efforts. Although social interaction during work hours between staff was discouraged, he did enjoy the occasional banter that he had with his adjacent work neighbour, Joe. Joe was younger than Spencer, dark-haired and fresh-faced, he still lived with his parents, and was single and carefree; his demeanour was that of somebody who lived for the moment and did not have the pressures in life that Spencer now experienced.

Joe popped his head above Spencer's cubicle.

'How's it going Spence?' he asked.

'Swimmingly,' replied Spencer, with a doomed air of sarcasm. 'You?'

Joe smiled, and nodded. 'Word on the street is there's going to be an announcement soon.'

'Oh great. Can't wait.'

'Looks like we're being taken over by AI.'

'Robots are taking over the world,' said Spencer, despairingly. 'I think there should be another Peasant's Revolt.'

'A what?'

'Never mind,' he replied, resignedly. His desk phone rang; he picked up the receiver and began the daily drudge of work routine.

Lying in bed that night, Spencer contemplated his future. If he was laid off, he would have to find another job. The thought of going through the rigmarole of interviews and rejections again sent him spiralling into a dark place. He seemed to be falling in a whirlpool of despondency. His mind ached with all the machinations of trying to rise above the external influences in his life which were outside of his control. He drifted off to sleep from sheer mental exhaustion.

Spencer didn't know where he was; all he knew was that the air was crisp and damp as he once again walked through soulless streets that seemed to lead to nowhere. It was the dead of night and eerily quiet. The only sound that he could hear was the sound of his own footsteps. Once again, he saw the occasional homeless person here and there, and the sight made him feel dispirited. He tried desperately to find something that would lead him back to familiar territory, but it was to no avail. Tall buildings seemed to look down upon him with disdain as he continued on his journey. He walked for miles before a familiar mist slowly began to fall.

As he continued walking, he stumbled across the entrance to what appeared to be an old disused railway station. The gates had been vandalised and were partly open. To escape the damp misty weather, he squeezed through the gap and let himself in. The building was vast. Clearly it was from a bygone era. It was very dusty and dirty but the ornate iron structure of the roof and its surroundings gave it an aura of old-world Victorian charm. Lit by faint moonlight through the high windows, Spencer could see the remains of two platforms in the distance; there was a ticket sales office and a waiting room nearby. He let himself into the dark waiting room and sat on one of the wooden benches.

'You look lost,' said an old man's familiar echoey voice from somewhere close to him.

Although Spencer was taken aback, he was determined to respond despite misgivings. 'I am,' he said, cautiously.

'Aren't we all?' said the old man.

'How do I get back?'

'How do any of us?'

Spencer was puzzled. 'I don't understand…'

'We all have to find our own way home.'

'Who *are* you?'

Spencer realised that he was once again all alone, and it was then that he awoke from his dream; he tried to make sense of it all but he couldn't find any. Who was that old man and what did his words mean? The dream always felt so real to Spencer, but of course it couldn't be… it was just a dream after all…

At work, later that afternoon, there was an announcement that they had all been dreading for so long; their services were no longer required. As predicted, the company was being taken over by AI. An atmosphere of gloom and despondency enveloped the office as they each began to vacate their working spaces for the last time.

As Spencer was about to finally leave the entrance to the office and venture out to an unknown world, Joe approached him.

'Can't say I'll miss this place,' he said.

'What will you do?' asked Spencer.

'Find another job, I guess. You?'

'Same, I suppose. Might take a while though. A lot of jobs are being taken up by AI. Doesn't seem fair, does it?'

'No. It's a regular balls-up. Not much we can do about it, is there?'

Spencer gave a downhearted sigh. 'No.'

Joe offered Spencer his hand; Spencer shook it warmly. 'Good luck Spence,' he said.

'All the best.'

Spencer watched Joe disappear into the distance. Life is funny, he mused: we're all just passing through. Part of life's rich tapestry... Joe was right, it *is* a regular balls-up. Technology was supposed to make things better, not worse... He felt a cloud of depression come over him, and his mood became increasingly sombre; it was then that he started to walk, not knowing, or caring, where he was going...

As minutes turned into hours, time seemed to stand still for Spencer, as he continued on his way. He felt the need to become invisible; to discard the travails of harsh economic reality: the pitfalls and pratfalls that had been thrust unwittingly upon him. His life suddenly felt... expendable.

Spencer found himself wondering in an area that he had never known before. Sights, sounds and smells that were new and alien to him. It was as if he was a stranger in a strange new world. Light faded into darkness, and he suddenly felt so completely alone. The desperate faces of sporadic homeless people could be seen in the gloom. Occasionally he would catch his reflection in a window: a long-haired bearded man in a dark suit, white shirt and scuffed shoes who would look back at him. How long had he been walking? Time was playing tricks on him. Surely, he was dreaming, but he knew deep down that he was not.

The air became chilly in the dead of night. Spencer lifted the lapel of his jacket to cover his neck, and put his hands in the pockets to keep the cold at bay. Where *was* he? A sense of isolation engulfed him; it was a feeling that he recognised from his dream.

Gradually, almost inevitably, a mist began to develop, and it hampered his view and his progress. Spencer sought sanctuary from the cold damp air in a nearby church that he stumbled upon. As he entered the building, and closed the door behind him, he saw a few lit candles at the far end which gave enough light to see the various sculptures of deceased dignitaries, from a bygone age, around the walls of the church. An effigy of religious significance looked down upon him from above as he now sat, in quiet contemplation, on one of the wooden benches. Although Spencer was not a religious man, as such, the aura within the church was powerfully spiritual. From somewhere close behind him came an old man's voice.

'You look lost.'

Spencer looked round but all he could discern was the dark silhouette of the old man.

'I am,' replied Spencer, emotionally.

'Aren't we all?' said the old man.

'How do I get back?'

'How do any of us?'

'I don't understand...'

'We all have to find our own way home.'

'Who *are* you?'

'That's not important,' replied the old man. 'The question you should ask yourself is: Who am *I*?'

'I know who *I* am.'

'Do you?' replied the old man.

'I'm Spencer Tate, and I'm... *lost*.'

'You've been walking in the dark for too long.'

Spencer let the old man's simple but profound words sink in. He was right. How can *anyone* find their way in the dark? Of *course* he was lost. 'You're right,' he said.

'You have a daughter who needs a father, no matter how hopeless life becomes.'

Spencer nodded his agreement. He turned to the old man. 'How did you-'
The old man's silhouette was nowhere to be seen…

Spencer opened the door to the church, and as he walked out to a new day, the glare from the sunlight dazzled his eyes. He bathed in the warmth of the light, and for once felt free from the anxiety that had plagued him for so long. It was a welcome relief to finally find clarity in a world that was once unrelentingly dark. He knew, from that moment on, that all would be well, in time, no matter what the circumstances may be.

On his journey home he saw his reflection in a window: a man in his thirties with neat, short blond hair, clean-shaven, wearing a dark suit and shiny black shoes. Spencer felt renewed, as though his life had new meaning.

As he continued on his journey, he thought about the old man and his simple but wise words. It was as if Spencer had glanced into the future and perhaps confronted his older self. How did he know that Spencer had a daughter? Why did he appear in his dream? There was something about the old man that seemed terribly familiar. But it couldn't be…

Could it…?

A Curious Reunion

The invitation came from out of the blue.

John Fanshaw sat at the table of his dining room, with his laptop open, and was checking his inbox for new emails when he spotted it. Simply titled *Reunion*, he could see that it was from Tim Stapleton, which was a name that he recognised from his schooldays of more than forty years ago; they had attended Moresham Secondary Modern School together, having failed their eleven plus exam, like so many others. It was a school known for being rough and ready, with teachers who were quick to dish out corporal punishment for even minor indiscretions, such as talking during class – a custom now frowned upon, but back then it was common practice.

Tim had managed to locate John and five others through social media, and suggested a get-together in a pub in London for old times' sake.

John looked at the other recipients of the email, and it brought back recollections of them as they were when they were together at school. They, like him, would probably be retired by now and look completely different. John glanced at himself in the mirror on the wall and decided that he had worn well despite the passing of too many years: he still had a full head of hair, although it was now silver, and had a kindly face. He could probably lose a few pounds, but even so… Despite being a widower of ten years, with back ache, dodgy knees, and occasional headaches, life had been good to him. Having worked in insurance for most of his working life, he had just about enough to get by on.

John let his mind drift back in time. Forty years… Where did it go? It only seemed like yesterday when he was at Moresham's. It wasn't a happy time or place to be. Why would anyone want to arrange a reunion from *that* school? On his last day at the school, he recalled, he literally ran home as fast as his legs would carry him. The happiest day at Moresham's was the day he left it… and yet… now that he thought about it… surely there must have been *some* days that were just about bearable…?

'*Fanny, get your head out of your arse!*'

It was the unmistakeable voice of Tim, and it was on the football pitch at school. It seemed that a lot of the pupils at school, including many of the teachers, called John *Fanny*. It was a misnomer that he would be plagued with for most of his school life. He wasn't a particularly good football player, and played as a defender. Tim berated him for letting the opposing forward score a goal without being effectively challenged. It was a tongue-lashing that was commonplace back then. John reminisced that they would play other schools, and a lot of pride was at stake. Tim was the captain of the school team, and did all he could to get the best out of a bad bunch; tall and athletic, he was the archetypal all-round athlete: good at all aspects of physical endeavour; unfortunately for him, nobody else shared his sporting prowess, and as a result he was in a league of his own.

They invariably lost…

Memories began to flood back in John's mind as he thought of his school days way back when; voices and events that had been locked away for so long were suddenly now clear and concise, as though it was only yesterday…

He took another look at the names of the other recipients: Paul Dunning, Robert Nadier, Ian Danser, Billy Sennet and Andrew Kilter. He could picture each of them when they were all in their mid-teens. He remembered sitting next to Paul Dunning, in a coach on a school trip to Leeds Castle in Kent. Paul had a ruddy-faced complexion and he was several pounds overweight for his age. As they sat on the coach, it was Paul who started the conversation, in hushed tones…

'Word to the wise…'
'What's that?'
'Tim's after your blood.'
'You've got to be sh-shitting me?'
Paul shakes his head.
'Puts all of our losses on the football pitch down to you.'
'I don't even like f-football.'
'I know. Me neither.'
'Why didn't you b-back me up?'
'Oh, I don't know… Self-preservation?'
'You're our goalie. Why doesn't he p-pick on you?'
Paul shakes his head.
'It's one of those mysteries in life, I suppose.'
'Well, that's just g-great. What can I do about it?'
'Keep out of his way, I guess.'
'Easier said than done when we're in the s-same class… Bollocks.'

John sat up straight, shocked by the stark realisation of his sudden recollection. It was as though he had travelled back in time; he felt the same sense of fear and dread as he did that day. He must have supressed those feelings all these years and somehow buried them. It was not a pleasant feeling. There was a lot of bullying that went on at Moresham's, and he now realised that he was an unfortunate victim. There were lots of fights in the playground back then when disputes between pupils were settled with fists. John was not a fighter, and others took advantage of his perceived weakness. Tim had bullied him on and off throughout his school days. He'd tried hard to laugh it off but, now that he thought about it, his life at school was pretty miserable. The teachers were just as bad. He remembered his physics teacher Mister Finnigan calling him to the front of the class for talking during a lesson…

'Fanshaw. Come here.'

John remembered those words as though they were now imprinted on his brain. Mister Finnigan was disabled, and used his walking cane to exact punishment. It was as though he was making up for his infirmity by taking it out on unruly pupils. Talking during class seemed such a stupid crime which, these days, may result in a mild ticking off – but back then it was a major misdemeanour.

John relived the embarrassment of walking to the front of the class, having to bend over on command, and receiving two thwacks on his rear by that bastard Finnigan. Other pupils in the class found the whole incident amusing, and he could still hear their stifled laughter. He wasn't sure which was worse – the punishment or the cruel mockery from his supposed peers.

It was a different world back then, thought John. There seemed to be a dog-eat-dog mentality within the confines of school life, from the top down. Even the headmaster seemed to take delight in extracting pain and humiliation from the punishment he inflicted upon insubordinate pupils. It was all very Dickensian but it was the late twentieth century, and not the nineteenth.

John remembered Robert Nadier as the class clown. Always quick with a joke and able to mimic the teachers and pupils with disarming accuracy, Robert was a popular boy at school, always smartly attired, and had good survival skills. Unfortunately, he would often imitate John's stutter to the great merriment of the other pupils. It always made John cringe with embarrassment. He remembered being in the school canteen, while they were eating their school lunch, and Robert sat opposite him…

'Pass the s-s-s-salt please F-F-Fanny.'
'That's not f-funny.'
Laughter from other pupils.
'Where's your sense of humour?'

'F-Fuck off Nadier.'

For retribution, John recalled, Robert flicked a pea at him. Not reacting was the best course of action, so John ignored him and carried on with his lunch. But inside, he felt worthless. School life gave him a cynical outlook on the world, which he took with him into the adult world. Thankfully, outdated attitudes and opinions changed in time, and people became more tolerant of those that were viewed as *different*. But back then... it was still neolithic.

Was his memory as accurate as he imagined? Could life at school have really been that bad, or was his aged mind playing tricks on him? He thought long and hard... yes, it really *was* that bad. He hadn't thought about school life for over forty years, and now that he had received that invitation from Tim, it was all he could *think* of. Others must have had different perceptions, otherwise why would he be invited to a reunion? Perhaps it was to rub salt in the wound, he speculated, but thought better of it. Life had taught him that people only remember what they want to remember, and delete memories that contravene their own prejudices. The truth of the matter was that his formative years at school were marred by others who somehow felt superior to him, and were not afraid to make their feelings known. Having a stutter was his Achilles heel, he realised, as well as his lack of athletic ability, and others were keen to exploit his perceived weakness. What should have been a time to look back on his schooldays with fond nostalgia, was now just a dark cloud from the past.

John remembered Ian Danser as the class creep. Skinny as a rake, with long black hair, Ian was so subservient to the teachers that he was known by the other pupils as Teacher's Pet. It was a survival strategy that backfired, because the other boys resented his eagerness to please, and as a consequence gave him a hard time. John recalled a geography lesson given by Mister Willet that landed him in trouble…

'*Who's talking back there? Danser, is that you?*'
'*No sir. It was Fanny.*'
'*Me?*'
'*Fanny. Front and centre.*'

Mister Willet was unique in the school, in that he was the only teacher that offered an unruly pupil the option to choose which size slipper, from a box of different sized slippers, he would prefer to be struck with. If you chose the smallest, Willet would put much greater effort in his swing to make up for the slipper's lack of substance. Barbaric… John could still recall the embarrassment and shame he felt when he was struck twice for such a minor offence. He felt like getting his revenge on Ian in the playground, but it wasn't really in his nature. Perhaps he was too forgiving, he thought. It was only when he was back at home that he used to seethe with anger, thinking about adverse past events. Maybe he should have been as cynical at the time as all the others; after all, the school was a melting pot of pettiness, vindictiveness and vitriol, which were the building blocks of cynicism. It was a vicious circle that encompassed all the negative attributes of human nature. It would take a long time for social and political attitudes to change, but by then the damage had already been done to the psyche of countless victims, he surmised, including himself...

Billy Sennet was short and had a fiery temper. Whether it was a Napoleon complex, or not, John wasn't sure, but he was a psycho when rattled, and many was the time when he lost it at the slightest provocation; John recalled one such incident that happened to him in the busy school hallway one lunchtime. John was making his way to the canteen when he bumped into Billy, and accidentally knocked the books out of his arm…

'*What the fuck?*'

'S-Sorry. Didn't see you.'
'Pick them up dipstick.'
'What?'
'You heard.'

Others stopped and stared. John picked up the books, and handed them back to Billy, who rushed past him, knocking him over in the process. All the others watching, laughed.

It was yet another humiliating experience during his schooldays that John now remembered as though it was yesterday.

Dark thoughts began to cloud his mind. He found it hard to visualise positive thoughts about his time at Moresham's, when so many days were spent in abject misery. Perhaps the school was cursed? Perhaps *he* was cursed? Either way, it was a bleak period in his life that he had conveniently filed away somewhere in the dark recess of his mind... and, in time, conveniently forgotten.

Andrew Kilter was the last of the recipients. John remembered Andrew as somebody who he thought was a friend but, when the chips were down, wouldn't hesitate to stab you in the back. Ginger-haired, with freckles to match, Andrew was a slight figure who looked as though a gust of wind would have blown him over. Figuratively speaking it was others' harsh words that blew away his confidence and caused him to betray a friendship in order to protect his own skin. John recalled just such an example: They were in the playground, during a break, minding their own business, and talking about a television programme that they had both seen the night before, when Andrew spotted a school thug by the name of Ken Cook fast approaching them. He made a beeline for Andrew...

'What you lookin' at?'
'Nothing.'

'Don't give me that shit. Fancy me or somethin', do you?'
'John was just saying here comes the school clown.'
'M-Me?'
Ken turns his attention to John.
'Oh... did you now?'
John didn't have time to deflect the punch from Ken that landed painfully on his nose; blood poured immediately from it onto the ground, as Ken slowly, but triumphantly, walked away.

It was just another example of an unpleasant day at Moresham's, John reflected. There seemed to be so many of them back then...

That evening, as John lay in bed trying to sleep, dark thoughts of his time at that school kept entering his mind. Visions that had lain forgotten for decades, now swirled like a whirlwind around him. Distorted familiar faces laughed and taunted him, like scenes from a horror film. Even as he fell into a deep sleep, he was plagued with nightmares of adverse situations that he recognised from his schooldays: punishments, bullying and harsh words from his peers; they scattered like leaves in a hellish inferno.

He awoke with a start.

The next few nights were the same...

That email from Tim had unlocked a Pandora's box of painful recollections that John now found difficult to ignore; it infiltrated his thoughts during the day, and tormented him during the night.

As he sat at his dining table, he looked once again at the email on his laptop, and made a decision: he was going to confront his demons, once and for all.

He clicked on *Reply all* and wrote: *See you there*. He then pressed *Send*.

It was the evening of the reunion, and as John approached The Hermit's Retreat pub in the City of London, he was feeling apprehensive, to say the least. What if they continued their taunts? By joining them was he going to be, once again, the butt of their snide remarks? How can something so long ago still have such a profound effect upon him? Perhaps by attending this reunion it would unlock even *more* unsavoury recollections that would haunt him forever more? With such bleak thoughts in his head, John summoned the courage, and entered the pub. It was a dark, almost gothic, area with a serving counter that seemed to stretch forever. There were wooden benches along the edges of the walls with alcoves, here and there, for private functions. It was from just such an alcove at the far end of the pub, that he heard an old man's voice that, although feeble, sounded strangely familiar.

'Fanny!'

He hadn't been called Fanny for over forty years. It felt unsettling to hear it again after all this time, and brought him back to a time he had preferred to forget. As he peered through the dimly-lit interior, and walked slowly towards the back of the building, it was then that he saw them: five elderly gentlemen gathered inside an alcove; one of them, who John belatedly realised was Tim Stapleton, was in a wheelchair, and it was his voice that he had heard.

'Long time no see, John. How the hell are you?'

Tim offered his hand to John, who shook it instinctively.

'I'm well, thanks.' John replied, feeling a pang of remorse.

'You remember these reprobates?' said Tim, gesturing to the others.

As John shook hands with the rest of them, he couldn't help but be silently astonished by how much they had all aged. Paul Dunning was still stout, seemed to have lost a number of teeth, and was supported by a walking cane. Robert Nadier, once a dapper popular pupil was now scruffily dressed, with white thinning hair, and had a dubious scent about him. Ian Danser was still slightly built, had a rapidly diminishing hairline, and wore glasses so thick that it made his eyes look miniscule. Billy Sennet was the shortest of the group, was as bald as a billiard ball, and tried to hold his protruding stomach in without much success. Andrew Kilter was still looking alarmingly fragile, and his once-ginger locks were now replaced with snow-white long hair tied up at the back.

It was a surreal experience to see faces that he remembered from when he was a child, who were now in their twilight years, as was he. This is what it must be like to be a time traveller, he thought. They were like ghosts from a period in his life that he had conveniently dismissed from his mind for so many years, and now... in a blink of an eye... here they were.

They all initially talked about their various ailments that had afflicted them in their old age. Tim had had a stroke a couple of years ago, which left him partially paralysed. Paul had suffered a heart attack, which had resulted in heart surgery. Robert was an alcoholic, and was now in remission. Ian was a recovering drug addict, and had been homeless for several years. Billy had high blood pressure and was diabetic. Andrew had mental health issues, and had been struggling with depression for the last decade.

John didn't feel the need to mention his own minor afflictions, as they paled into insignificance compared to the others'. Time had not been kind to them, and he felt compassion begin to swell within him, despite historic grievances that he had held for all these years. Belatedly, he now realised that people change over the years and become something other than what they once were.

As the evening wore on, and the drinks began to flow, John excused himself and went to the gents to splash some water upon his face; he had a nagging headache that seemed to consume him. Whether it was the stress of seeing old adversaries from so long ago, he wasn't sure. Perhaps it was guilt?

As he looked himself in the mirror, with water trickling down his face, a familiar feeling of despair engulfed him. It had been ten long years since his wife had passed away from breast cancer, and the pain of loneliness since then had been palpable. Some days had been unbearable, and he wondered how he had survived the years that followed. It had been a profound time in his life, and the absence of friends, long since gone, or of any visitors, had left him bereft.

As he came back out into the pub lounge, John returned to the dark alcove, which was now void of any human life, and he realised… yet again… that his mind had once more created an alternative reality which had seemed so convincingly factual. Tears welled in his eyes as he began his long, lonely, walk home…

As John sat at the table of his dining room, with his laptop open, he was checking his inbox for new emails, when he saw a new message…

A Chance Encounter

Abbey Park Cemetery, July 1963
Jessica Dobson is sat alone on an old wooden bench, in the heart of Abbey Park Cemetery, situated in East London. It was a warm sunny day, and she often came here, as she found it an agreeable place to sit and immerse herself in the calm serenity and tranquillity that the area seemed to exude. The sun felt good on her elderly pale face, and the bench provided temporary comfort for her weary bones. Her plain black dress soaked up the sun's rays, and she basked in its pleasing glow.

Although the cemetery was now largely overgrown with plants, trees, and wild shrubbery, she found an inner peace in her solitude here that she hadn't really felt elsewhere throughout her long life.

As Jessica looked out to her surroundings, she was struck by how beautiful the world could be, despite the trials and tribulations that seemed to always inhabit the human way of life. A slight wind rustled in the trees; it was as if nature was talking to her and saying: *'You are welcome here'*.

Thinking back on her youth, as she often did, she remembered a time of struggle and hardship that many others also had to endure during a bleak period of austerity. As a young girl, her education was cut short, and she was sent to work in a textile factory to help support the family's welfare. Her father was unable to work because of an injury he had sustained during the course of his employment as a railway fitter. It was Jessica and her mother who were now the breadwinners of the family. After a few years working at the factory, Jessica met and befriended a young man by the name of Arthur, who helped maintain the machinery needed for the production of the cotton fabric the factory produced. It was a welcome relief from the drudgery of daily life to have found a friendly face. Arthur was tall for his eighteen years of age, ebony-skinned, and handsome, and they were soon taken with each other. They would often arrange to meet in secret in the local park, where they would walk, hand in hand, and promise their undying love for each other. This was all a new experience for Jessica, as she was still unschooled in the matters of the heart, but it felt right, and she embraced their new-found attachment with abandonment.

As their friendship developed, and time wore on, Jessica fell pregnant. She had no idea of the controversy of being with child at such a young age, and her parents strongly chastised her; she was sent away to have the baby which was then to be adopted. Despite Arthur's fervent protestations, he was ostracised by the community, and was forbidden by his parents to see Jessica ever again.

When Jessica gave birth to her son, he was immediately taken away from her by the nurse, and disappeared forever from her life. The experience left Jessica feeling hollow, and she never overcame the pain of loss that she felt at that moment. For the rest of her days, she remained single and unwilling to allow her feelings to lead her into a committed relationship.

When she returned to the family home, she soon found work as a domestic servant for a large family; they paid a pittance for a salary, but she had board and lodging which meant a roof over her head with meals included. She sent most of her money to her parents to help them in their need. Daily life working as a domestic servant was hard work: up at the crack of dawn cleaning, washing, emptying the grates in the fireplace, and lighting the fire when it was cold. Then she would help the cook in the kitchen. It was a thankless job, but she was grateful to be regularly employed.

As the years went by, and she became middle-aged, both of her parents died shortly after one another, and Jessica found herself living alone in the compact terraced family home that she had inherited after their passing. She made a small income as a cleaner in the local area, and kept herself to herself until she retired in her later years.

Jesssica's train of thought was interrupted by the approach of a distinguished looking elderly man, supported by a walking cane in his right hand; he was tall, olive-skinned, and had a full head of white hair. He was smartly dressed in a dark suit, white shirt and blue tie, shiny black shoes, and had the bearing of an old soldier. In his left hand, he carried a full plastic bag.
  'Would you mind if I joined you, madam?' he asked.
  Jessica was pleasantly surprised at the elderly man's politeness, and gestured to the space beside her on the bench. 'You're perfectly welcome,' she said.
  He lowered himself carefully onto the bench, put the bag down onto the ground, and stretched his legs out.
  'Terrible thing… getting old,' he declared, wearily.
  'Inevitable, I'm afraid,' replied Jessica, smiling. 'Happens to the best of us.'
  'Indeed, it does,' he said, sadly. 'In the blink of an eye, as well. Soon as your back is turned, Mother Nature digs her claws into you.'
  Jessica felt a little taken aback by his interpretation of ageing. 'I must admit I hadn't thought of it quite like that, but time does go by quickly. Yes.'
  'But at the time…'
  Jessica waited for him to finish his sentence, but it lay undisturbed and incomplete for quite a while. There seemed to be an air of melancholy about him which she found strangely appealing. 'Do you live nearby?' she asked.
  'Oh no,' he replied. 'I live in Essex.'

'And what brings you here?'

The elderly man looked pensive in his response. 'I come here once a year. To pay my respects... I've been coming for the past sixteen years... Not many left I wouldn't wonder...'

Jessica could sense the sorrow in his voice, and tried to lift his spirit. 'If it's any consolation, you look as though you have many years still to enjoy.'

He smiled warmly. 'Looks can be deceptive, I'm afraid,' he said, gently. 'And how about you?'

'Hmm?'

'Do *you* live nearby?'

'Oh... yes,' she replied. 'I'm very close.'

'Then you are fortunate indeed. It's a welcome oasis in a world of madness.'

Jessica smiled at his analogy. 'Yes... You're right. I feel at home here...'

A poignant quietness ensued which did not seem out of place. It was the elderly man who spoke first.

'The Beatles seem to be everywhere at the moment,' he said. It's Beatles this... Beatles that. You can't turn on the radio without hearing their music.'

Jessica had no idea who the Beatles were. 'I prefer dance music myself. Glenn Miller is such a treat.'

'Now you're talking. *Real* music...'

They sat in silence for a long time looking out at their surroundings, absorbed in this moment in time together. They felt curiously comfortable in each other's company, as though they had known each other for years. There was something about this elderly man, thought Jessica, that seemed to resonate with her, but she didn't know why... It was Jessica who punctured the long silence. 'Do you have family in Essex?' she asked.

'I have a son,' he replied.

'It must be nice when he visits you?'

The elderly man had a sad look in his eyes. 'He keeps himself to himself,' he said. 'I hardly ever see him.'

'What a shame.'

'We fell out some years ago, over something trivial. These things happen, I suppose. I think I have a gruff nature. The army tends to take its toll on one's nerves... I'm afraid I have a rather short fuse.'

'You don't suffer fools gladly?'

He smiled stoically. 'Never have. So used to barking out orders, I've forgotten how to be... *normal*,' he confided.

Jessica felt his internal anguish, and a compassion slowly grew within her. After all, she knew what it was like to be cast aside. 'I'm sure you can settle your differences... in time. They say that time is a great healer.'

'Time would seem to be in short supply,' he said, defeatedly. 'He knows where I live. If he wants to see his old dad, he would be perfectly welcome.'

'Perhaps, if you were to make the first move...?'

The elderly man considered Jessica's proposal at length. 'You know...' he said. 'I believe you may be right. I shall make a point of it when I return home to call on him, and make amends while I'm still able.'

'That's the spirit. Life is too short to leave things unsaid, after all.'

'You're very perceptive,' he said, kindly.

'I've learned from experience it's better to forgive and forget... no matter what life throws at you.'

'I can tell you've had your own share of... *disappointment*.'

Jessica felt strongly inclined to change the subject, after a moment's painful recollection. 'You were in the army?'

He hesitated before answering. 'Yes... until shrapnel took me out of the war. It was at the battle of the Ancre along the Western Front. I was an officer in the Fifth Army.'

'You must have seen some terrible sights?'

'Indeed, I did... So many fallen comrades... Such a waste of young life. Ours *and* theirs... All because of incompetent politicians... And, blow me down, it happens again, twenty-five years later!' He shakes his head, disconsolately. 'Such a tragic waste...'

'Wars are so senseless...'

'I used to think that wars were a necessary evil, but after years of conflict, I firmly agree with you.'

Jessica could see the sorrow glisten in his eyes. 'It's the wisdom of old age,' she said, soothingly.

The elderly man smiled and nodded, sagely.

'When you're young, you have a different perspective on life,' he said. 'Things seem more black and white. When I was young, I couldn't wait to sign up and fight for my country. It seemed the right thing to do... But now... I realise the futility of it all. If governments talked to each other more, and maintained a friendly relationship, wars would be a thing of the past.'

'History has a tendency of repeating itself.'

'Indeed, it does... It's the frailty of the human endeavour, I'm afraid.'

Just then, a nightingale sang from one of the nearby trees; its beautiful rendition lightened an otherwise air of melancholy between the two of them, and lifted their spirits.

'It's so nice to hear birdsong, isn't it?' said Jessica. 'It reminds you that there are other creatures enjoying life, as well as ourselves.'

'I agree. We get so wrapped up in our own little worlds that we forget that we are just one of countless other species in this glorious existence.'

'It *is* glorious, isn't it?' said Jessica, affirmably. 'I feel quite at home here.'

They sat, in unison, listening to the sounds of nature all around them, and it was as if a heavy weight had been lifted from their shoulders. They bathed in the glory of their surroundings, and felt at peace in each other's company, for this unique moment in time, and negative emotions seemed to melt away as they absorbed the allure of this enchanted location.

'We are surrounded by the remains of the dead… and yet… life is still here for all to see and hear,' declared the elderly man, philosophically.

'Some people choose not to hear it. I think that is why there is so much sadness in the world. We are all just passing through, after all.'

'Time is a strange beast… I've lived a long life. When you are young, the thought of being old one day doesn't even occur to you. Sometimes, when I look in the mirror, I barely recognise my own reflection, and yet I know that that is who I have become…'

'It's a reality that we all have to come to terms with… in time… If we are lucky.'

'Part of life's rich tapestry?'

Jessica smiled knowingly, and nodded her agreement. 'Does the thought of your own mortality worry you?' she asked, caringly.

The elderly man pondered Jessica's question at length.

'I have seen death during battle many times, and at the time accepted it as part of the inevitability of war,' he said. 'But… until recently… I have never considered my own passing.'

'And now?'

'I have come to realise that I am at the extremity of my existence in this world.'

'And you have come to terms with it?'

A sadness filled the air with the elderly man's quiet contemplation.

'When my wife died five years ago, I would have welcomed death as a blessed relief. But now... as I sit here with you... I realise how precious life is.'

'I'm sure your wife would have been the first to agree with you.'

'Yes... you know, now that I come to think of it... I'm sure she would,' he said. 'She was a beacon in a world of darkness. I will always miss her.'

'Of course...'

'And you?'

'Hmm?'

'Are you married?' he asked. He could sense that she felt uncomfortable. 'I'm sorry. I didn't mean to pry...'

'Not at all,' said Jessica, who had never been asked that question before. 'I've lived a fairly solitary life,' she said.

'Sometimes it's nice to be in one's own company,' he said, kindly.

'It's been my choice to be alone. I've become so used to it that it's become a way of life, I suppose. There are times when I have regrets, but you make your own bed and you have to lie in it.'

'Indeed, you do...'

'If life has taught me anything, it's that you have to make the most of every day. As best you can.'

He arose from the bench, and picked up his bag. 'Wise words, indeed,' he said. 'I will take a leaf out of your book, I do believe. And now I must get on... Madam, it's been a pleasure meeting with you. I feel somehow rejuvenated in your company. Perhaps our paths will cross again?'

Jessica smiled. 'I rather think they will,' she said, softly.

As he walked away, Jessica felt at peace with the world. She wasn't sure why, but meeting that elderly man made her feel complete; as though a void was somehow filled... like the final piece in a jigsaw.

Walking down the gravel path, James stopped and turned around for one last glance at the delightful lady he had just met, but the bench was now conspicuously vacant. Feeling sad that he had never asked for her name, he resumed his journey, looking for the grave that he had visited loyally for the last sixteen years. Thoughts of the joys of life filled his heart as he walked along the path, and he found himself in a positive state of mind – something that of late had been missing in his life. His doctor had given him his dreadful diagnosis, but now he took it in his stride, knowing inside that this would be the last time that he would be able to visit this place of enchantment.

He took out a small watering can from his bag, filled it with water from a nearby tap, and then approached the gravestone with a heavy heart.

Weeds and ivy had engulfed the flat gravestone, and its words could not be seen. James knelt down, carefully pulled at all the growth and removed it as best he could, and sprinkled the stone with water. He took out a small brush from his bag and began meticulously brushing the stone. As he was doing this he was thinking of the gravestone's occupant. It was only late in his life that he discovered the identity of his real mother. He had never known her, but being beside this gravestone at this time, more than ever, he suddenly felt a special bond that had eluded him for so many years. He finished brushing, stood up, and with tears welling in his eyes, looked proudly at the result of his efforts:

Here Lies
Jessica Mary Dobson
Born 4th November 1871
Died 8th July 1946

Murder in Act Two

Albert Sandbury is sat watching the concluding act of the dress rehearsal of his Edwardian period play, *A Family in Conflict*, from front of house. As writer/director/stage manager, it was his job to ensure that everything was in good order, and performed as efficiently as an amateur production could be. He made notes of any glitches he noticed for last-minute adjustments, but ultimately the Summerhouse Players had had quite enough rehearsals, and he didn't want to jinx the occasion with too much negativity, as it would likely impair the quality of their performance. He wrote the play in his late twenties, and had kept it in a drawer for the past fifteen years, thinking that it would never see the light of day again, but when he heard that The Summerhouse Players were looking for new work, he approached them with his play. Their last director had quit due to *artistic differences*, and Albert bridged the gap quite nicely. Having never directed a stage play in his life, he managed to convince the others that he was up to the job from sheer bravado. He had studied dramatic arts at college, and came across as confident and efficient, and his play received the thumbs-up from the rest of the cast. In his professional life Albert was an accountant for a textile company, but his pipe dream had always been to be a successful playwright.

Albert took off his thick black-rimmed glasses, which made him resemble the actor Michael Caine in his prime, and rubbed at his tired eyes. It had been a stressful three weeks of read-throughs, bickering, and re-writes before the play was finally ready for performance at the Twixton Arts Theatre in South East Kent; it was a small local theatre with just over a hundred seats, but it was snug and had great acoustics for performances. The stage was set as a dining room of an affluent Edwardian mansion, somewhere in the North of England. The two acts of the play centres on a family gathering, following the funeral service of their elderly dearly-departed patriarch, Joseph Franklyn; it portrays the dynamics of a family at odds with each other, culminating in the suicide, by poison, of the deceased's eldest son, Gerald Franklyn, played by Alex Harding.

Alex Harding... As Albert thought of all the members of The Summerhouse Players, Alex was easily the most argumentative actor within the company; an actor who didn't like direction, criticism of any kind, and especially didn't like Albert; despite all of that, Alex was a competent actor. The rest of the cast were much easier to work with: Laurence Bigley, sixties, playing George Franklyn (brother of deceased), was larger than life, amiable, and the eldest member of the company; Stephanie Carruthers, fifties, playing Mary Franklyn (wife of George), was a seasoned progressive actress, always open to new ideas and direction; Tina Stapleton, forties, playing Beverley Franklyn, widowed mother, (daughter of George) was a passionate actress able to portray raw emotion; Debbie Pinkton, thirteen, playing Beverley's daughter, was the youngest member of the Summerhouse Players, who dreamed of a professional stage career; Ian King, whose family originated from Nigeria, was in his early twenties, playing Roger Franklyn (adopted son of Gerald), was studying drama at college, and took to acting like a duck to water; Tim Quinton, late twenties, playing Michael Franklyn (Roger's younger brother) was a fairly new member of the cast and still learning the ropes; Walter Delaney, thirties, playing Peter Henley (friend of Roger), had played many supporting roles for the company, and was a skilled actor.

The final scene was now in progress. Alex Harding had the stage to himself, and was about to deliver his final monologue, culminating in the suicide, by poison, of his character Gerald Franklyn.

Despite Albert's misgivings of Alex's negative attitude, he had to give him credit for a powerful performance. He watched, transfixed, as Alex delivered his last lines of the play:

'Who am I to live, when the man who raised me, and had such high hopes for my future, had his own life cut mercilessly short. I am not worthy to carry the family name, as I have not accomplished my father's ambition for me to follow in his esteemed footprints into the business of law. I have failed in my endeavours and have squandered the opportunities provided me with utmost contempt, through selfish enterprise.' He retrieves a small bottle from the inside of his jacket, and takes off its lid. 'My life has no meaning. I forfeit my existence from this intolerable burden.'

Gerald Franklyn downs the contents of the bottle, grabs at his throat in his final death throes, and collapses to the floor. The stage curtain closes. End of play.

Albert rises to his feet, in awe at such a magnificent performance, and shouts: 'Bravo! Bravo!' clapping thunderously in the process.

As the curtain re-opens, Alex is still lying motionless in the middle of the stage. *This is amazing,* thought Albert. *What a performance! What an actor!*

It was only when others rushed onto the stage and tried to resuscitate Alex, that Albert realised there was a problem.

Stephanie Carruthers, who had experience in these matters, gave Alex CPR and then the kiss of life; after a long while she turned to the others, solemnly, and declared: 'I'm afraid he's dead…'

Phillip Foray carefully examined the deceased's body that still lay undisturbed on the stage. Dressed formally in a tweed suit, white shirt, blue tie and brown shoes, Foray was the epitome of a country gentleman medical doctor. As a forensic pathologist it was his job to determine cause of an unexpected death that may or may not have been the result of foul play. The heat in the theatre was such that beads of sweat formed on his bald head; he mopped his brow with a handkerchief, careful to not allow any droplets to fall onto the deceased and taint evidence in the process. This would be one of the last cases he would be involved with before finally retiring.

DCI Jill Summersby and DI Paul Jenkins stood before the deceased, as Foray conducted his initial review before the body would be taken away for a formal post-mortem examination. The Summerhouse Players were seated, front of house, in a row, as instructed, while preliminary investigations were taking place; their details had been ascertained, and each had had their DNA and fingerprints taken.

'First impressions?' asked Summersby.

Foray looked up at the tall figure before him. DCI Summersby was relatively young for a senior rank, and her long blond hair belied the judicious professional police officer that she had become. DI Jenkins, on the other hand, was much shorter, and his closely-clipped dark brown hair somehow gave the impression of somebody who was born to be a police officer. Both wore long dark coats over their formal attire.

'My first impression is that this man has almost certainly been poisoned,' said Foray. 'Judging by the pallor of his skin, and traces of vomit around his blue lips, it must have been a fast-acting compound that penetrated and immobilised his vital organs. Of course, until I conduct a thorough examination in the lab, it's pure conjecture at this point in time pending the results of various tests. We'll examine the remains of the bottle used by Mister Harding.' Foray covered the body with a sheet.

Summersby turned to Jenkins. 'What do we know about the deceased?' she asked.

Jenkins consulted his notepad. 'Alex Harding, forty-three, no next of kin. Worked for the local supermarket as manager. Had been with The Summerhouse Players for the last ten years.'

'Have a look backstage. See if you can find the origin of the poison used. It may have been an accident, but it's more than likely to have been foul play. Take Doctor Foray with you. Use gloves.'

'Yes ma'am,' said Jenkins, efficiently. He turned and made his way backstage with Foray.

Summersby turned to The Summerhouse Players. 'Who's in charge?'

Albert sheepishly raised his hand. 'That would be me, I suppose,' he said.

Summersby beckoned Albert to the stage. As Albert made his way, Foray's two medical assistants carefully placed the dead body on a gurney, before wheeling it away.

When Albert was standing beside Summersby, she asked, discreetly: 'Can you think of anyone within the company that would intentionally harm Mister Harding?'

The question took Albert by surprise. 'I... err... I mean to say...'

'I appreciate this is a difficult time for you.'

'Difficult?' he said. 'I've never dealt with a corpse before. Corpsing, perhaps...'

Summersby didn't understand the theatrical term, and the brief moment of light relief was lost on her. 'I'm sorry?'

'Never mind… Alex Harding was quite a disagreeable person, all things considered, but I can't think of anyone who would want to *murder* him.'

Summersby considered Albert's statement at length before replying. 'In what way was he disagreeable?' she asked.

'Not the warmest of people, shall we say?' He thought about adding *certainly not now* but felt the humour would be lost on DCI Summersby.

'We will need to interview each member of the cast. Is there a room in the theatre that we can use?'

'There's a small office in the rear. You could use that.'

Just then, DI Jenkins and Doctor Foray re-entered the stage. Jenkins was holding what appeared to be a bottle of apple juice in his gloved hands.

'Doctor Foray believes this is the same liquid that Mister Harding used for his final scene,' said Jenkins.

'Same distinctive smell,' declared Foray. He opened up a plastic bag, and Jenkins carefully placed the bottle inside, and then Foray sealed it. 'I'll let you know its contents as soon as I can,' he said, and with that he departed stage-left.

The office in the theatre was cramped, to say the least. Albert sat on one side of the small wooden desk, and Summersby and Jenkins sat opposite him; Jenkins took notes as the meeting progressed.

'You're fairly new to The Summerhouse Players, Mister Sandbury?' asked Summersby.

'Please… call me Albert. Yes... I joined just a few months ago.'

'And what was the circumstance of you becoming director, as well as writer?'

'As I understand it Robert Panning, the previous director, left because he didn't feel he was valued.'

'Oh? In what way?'

'You'll have to ask somebody else, I'm afraid. I don't really know.'

Summersby thought this over and turned to Jenkins. 'Make a note to find out more about Robert Panning.'

Jenkins nodded without looking up from his note-taking.

Summersby returned her attention to Albert. 'Tell me about your impression of Alex Harding,' she said. 'What type of person was he?'

'Alex was a fine actor,' he said. 'Somewhat overbearing, but-'

'Overbearing? In what way?'

'Well... I don't like speaking ill of the dead...'

Summersby smiled sympathetically. 'Albert,' she said. 'You can speak freely here. This is just a preliminary interview to determine basic facts in our investigation. You understand that?'

'Yes... of course. Alex had a disagreeable temper. For some reason he disliked me from the beginning. But then again, he didn't seem to hit it off with *anybody*.'

'If he was as disagreeable as you say, why was he allowed to continue to perform for The Summerhouse Players?'

'That's easy,' said Albert. 'Because he was such a good actor, despite his temperament. We all knew that, and accepted his... *rough*... demeanour.'

'Can you think of anyone who would want to do Mister Harding harm?'

Albert considered at length before hesitantly replying. 'No...' he said. 'Of course not...'

The interview continued, in the same vein, until it came to its natural conclusion.

Summersby turned to Jenkins. 'Who's next on the list?'

Jenkins consulted his notepad. 'Laurence Bigley,' he said.

Summersby turned back to Albert. 'That will be all for now, Mister Sandbury. Could you ask Mister Bigley to come in please? Please remain front of house for now until all interviews are conducted.'

Albert nodded, and left the room...

Laurence is sat opposite Summersby and Jenkins; he was the elder statesman of The Summerhouse Players, flamboyant in his mannerisms, and eloquent in his speech. With his long silver hair, full matching beard, and still dressed in his Edwardian costume (as were all members of the cast), he gave off the aura of a seasoned theatrical performer.

'Will this take long?' he asked. 'I have another pressing engagement later this evening.'

'Mister Bigley,' said Summersby, rather impatiently. 'We are investigating the mysterious death of your colleague Alex Harding. I'm afraid it will take as long as is necessary.'

Laurence gave a sigh of resignation. 'Very well,' he said, and with that gave an exuberant gesture with his hand for Summersby to continue.

'Do you still work Mister Bigley?'

'Heavens no. I retired about ten years ago. I was a barrister.'

'And how do you pass the time?'

'I keep myself very busy. I'm a keen gardener, and of course the acting keeps me on my toes.'

'You've been with The Summerhouse Players for how long?'

'Since its inception. About thirty years, I suppose. You see, I was one of the founding members.'

'You must have seen a lot of people come and go?'

Laurence smiled. 'Oh yes... I am the only surviving original member.'

'What was your relationship with Alex Harding like?'

'I admired his acting ability, if not his character.'

'Oh? What was it about his character that you didn't approve of?'

'His coarse nature. I don't suffer fools, but Alex... Let's just say that he was not an easy man to get on with.'

'Can you think of anyone who would want to harm Mister Harding?'

Laurence gave Summersby's question long consideration before answering. 'I can't imagine any of the company resorting to murder, no.'

'But he was the most unpopular member of The Summerhouse Players?'

'Without question.'

Summersby hesitated before asking the next question. 'What can you tell me about Mister Harding's working relationship with Robert Panning?'

Laurence's face turned suddenly pale, and his eyes became sad. 'It was very unfortunate. They had an... *altercation.*'

'In what way?'

'Robert was trying to give Alex direction. It was during rehearsal for *Who's Afraid Of Virginia Woolf.* It got very ugly.'

Summersby's curiosity was piqued. 'Did they come to blows?'

Laurence shook his head. 'Very nearly. I had to intervene, otherwise...'

'And Mister Panning left the company as a result?

'After the play was performed, yes.' Laurence's eyes became downcast. 'Most regrettable. What goes around...'

Summersby could see that Bigley was feeling distressed, and so only asked a few more questions before concluding the interview. Stephanie Carruthers was next on the list...

Stephanie sat patiently, waiting for the interview to commence. She had a kindly face, and meticulously brushed back a loose strand of her flowing auburn hair from her forehead, while in attendance.

'Miss Carruthers, how long have you been a member of The Summerhouse Players?' asked Summersby.

'Oh, I'd say I joined when I was about thirty... almost twenty years ago now.' She smiled as she re-lived the moment in her head.

Summersby's eyes raised slightly, as she was sure that Carruthers was nearer sixty than fifty, but she didn't pursue it... for now. 'What was your relationship with the deceased like?'

'Alex? I didn't dislike him as much as everyone else did. Having said that, I was not a fan because of his disrespect to all of us.'

'And yet you were the first to attend to him when he collapsed.'

'Why, yes. Of course. I was a nurse in my professional life.'

'Was?'

'Before I retired... *early*.'

Summersby nodded knowingly. 'Miss Carruthers, can you think of anyone within The Summerhouse Players who would want Mister Harding dead?'

Stephanie looked aghast at the suggestion. 'Good lord, no. But then...'

'Yes?'

'If you had asked me that question several months ago, I would have suggested Robert Panning as a likely suspect.'

Summersby turned to Jenkins. 'Make a note to interview Mister Panning.' Jenkins nodded affirmatively. She then returned her attention to Stephanie. 'I take it they didn't see eye to eye?'

'It got very ugly. I thought there would be fisticuffs, but thankfully Laurence interceded and calmed the situation before it got out of control.'

'It seems that Mister Bigley, despite his age, was quite the peacemaker.'

'Robert was about the same age as Laurence.' Stephanie hesitated before adding: 'Laurence has always been protective of all members of The Summerhouse Players.'

'So it would seem… I only have a few more questions for you Miss Carruthers…'

Ian King is sat patiently in attendance within the office, waiting for the interview to commence. DCI Summersby and DI Jenkins were reviewing the notes taken so far, and quietly communicating their thoughts between themselves before turning their attention to him.

'Mister King, you are one of the youngest members of The Summerhouse Players, is that correct?'

'Yes,' he replied. 'Debbie, at thirteen, is obviously the youngest. Then me. I'm studying drama at uni. I have another couple of years before I graduate. I hope to pursue a career in the arts.'

Summersby could see that King was probably about twenty years of age. He had the appearance of somebody who was bitten by the acting bug. He was attentive, intelligent, and responsive. 'How would you describe your relationship with Mister Harding?'

Ian looked despondent. 'He was very patronising,' he said. 'And a narcissist…'

Summersby could sense King was very uncomfortable, but pursued her line of inquiry. 'That must have been very upsetting for you?'

Ian nodded silently. 'You have no idea. But I didn't kill him.'

'Mister Harding didn't seem to have many positive attributes? It makes one wonder how he lasted as long as he did within the company.'

'That's easy,' said Ian. 'He was a consummate actor. They say that Brando was difficult to work with. I think that Alex was out of that same mould. I'm sure he could have been a professional if he had played his cards better.'

'Interesting... So, despite all of your reservations of Mister Harding, you still have a modicum of respect for his acting abilities?'

'Absolutely. As a student of drama, I can tell a good actor from a ham.'

'A *ham*?'

'Somebody who overacts... Like Laurence, perhaps?'

'I see... How do you get on with the rest of The Summerhouse Players, Mister King?'

'I get on well with all of The Summerhouse Players,' he declared. 'I try to be as professional as I can, despite my own minor misgivings...'

Tina Stapleton and Debbie Pinkton are sat huddled next to each other, awaiting DCI Summersby's questions.

Tina theatrically stifled a yawn as she was waiting. Summersby could tell that she was impatient, and perhaps a little on edge. Debbie, despite her youth, sat patiently without a care in the world.

'Thank you both for coming in. I'm sure this won't take long,' said Summersby. 'I thought it best, Miss Stapleton, given Miss Pinkton's youth, that she be accompanied by an adult.'

'Given that I'm her mother, it makes perfect sense,' said Tina, surreptitiously.

Summersby was slightly taken aback, and turned to Jenkins.

'I'm on it,' said Jenkins, stringently taking notes.

Summersby turned her attention back to Tina. 'I had no idea,' she said. 'Is Pinkton a stage name?'

'No,' said Tina, dismissively.

Summersby made a mental note to pursue this at a later date. 'How long have you both been members of The Summerhouse Players?'

'About five years,' said Tina, and turned to her daughter.

'Coming up to two years,' said Debbie.

'And do you hope to be a professional actress in the future, Miss Pinkton?'

'That would be a dream come true,' she replied. 'If I can get into RADA when I'm eighteen, then I will be very happy.'

Tina resolved to play devil's advocate with her daughter. 'It's incredibly difficult, not to say expensive to join RADA. Only the very best can study there.'

'Then I will have to be the best actress in the world, mummy,' she replied.

Tina smiled lovingly at her daughter's aspiration, and then gave a long sigh. Summersby could sense the sorrow underlying her façade.

'Can either of you think of anyone within The Summerhouse Players who would wish harm upon Mister Harding?'

Summersby noticed a distinct pause before Stapleton responded.

'No...'

Tim Quinton sat opposite DCI Summersby and DI Jenkins, calmly surveying the confined room he now found himself in. It was a messy room, he thought. 'It's a good job I'm not claustrophobic,' he declared to himself, lightly.

'It will do for now, Mister Quinton. Tell me, how long have you been with The Summerhouse Players?'

'About a year, I suppose.'

'Were you with a different theatre company before you joined here?'

'Yes. I was a member of The Sugosi Theatre Company for about three years.'

'And what made you leave?'

'I work for a pharmaceutical company in London that moved to within ten miles of Twixton, so it made sense to up sticks and move closer to here.'

Summersby's attention was piqued. 'I see... And how long have you worked there?'

'Since leaving uni about ten years ago. I have a masters in Chemistry so I thought I'd put it to good use.'

'What was your relationship with Mister Harding like?'

Tim looked agitated before responding. 'He was a bully,' he said.

'Oh? And why do you think that was?'

Summersby could sense Quinton's discomfort.

'I think he was intimidated by those he perceived as... *different*.'

'In what way, Mister Quinton?'

'He was homophobic...'

Walter Delaney was the last on the list to be interviewed. As he sat waiting, Walter crossed his arms, impatiently, and eyed DCI Summersby and DI Jenkins with instinctive misgiving. Diminutive in stature, and with ginger hair, Walter had learned how to be assertive from an early age.

'Mister Delaney, how long have you been a member of The Summerhouse Players?' asked Summersby.

'A few years now.'

'And do you work nearby?'

Walter felt uneasy. 'I'm currently unemployed,' he said.

'Oh? How do you support yourself?'

'I live with my parents.' Walter's eyes narrowed. 'Is that a problem?'

'Not at all. What was your relationship with Mister Harding like?'

Walter considered at length before responding. 'I probably got on with him better than the others. He liked to gamble, as do I.'

'The horses?'

Walter nodded. 'He was a terrible gambler. He still owes me. Borrowed quite a bit of money off me. Don't suppose I'll ever see that again.'

Summersby viewed Delaney with some suspicion. 'And where did you get the money from to lend to Mister Harding?'

Walter gave a slight smirk. 'I buy and sell. Here and there. Sort of a hobby of mine, you might say?'

'I note from initial inquiries that you have a criminal record?'

Walter's smirk faded. 'That was a long time ago,' he said, despondently.

'And what was that for, may I ask?'

Walter hesitated before responding. 'Possession.'

Summersby and Jenkins are sat in the office on their own, reviewing the interview notes taken.

'What are your first thoughts?' asked Summersby.

'Most of the cast would seem to have a reason to bump Harding off,' he said. 'Although there seems to be a general underlying respect for his acting ability.'

Summersby nodded. 'I agree. Motive is the key to this. If he was murdered, and it seems likely, it had to be a deeply personal reason. Do a detailed background check on each member of The Summerhouse Players. I'll look into the deceased and see if there's anything we've missed. See if you can get Mister Panning's side of the story. There may be more to this than meets the eye.'

Jenkins nodded affirmatively. 'Where's Agatha Christie when you need her?'

'Indeed.'

Back at the station, two days later, with coffee in hand, DCI Summersby was scrutinising the link board on the wall that showed pictures of each member of The Summerhouse Players; beneath each picture was a synopsis giving brief background details. In the middle of the board was the deceased Alex Harding. How can one person be so unpopular, she thought, and yet still command a modicum of respect for his prowess on the stage? She had uncovered some interesting facts about Mister Harding which may or may not give a motive for his sudden demise, but for now kept it to herself.

DI Jenkins walked in in an excited state, interrupting Summersby's thoughts.

'Panning topped himself about six months ago,' he said, breathlessly. 'And you'll never guess where he lived, and with whom.'

Jenkins showed the evidence from his notebook, when the phone rang.

Summersby answered the phone. It was Foray. As she listened to what he had to say, her eyes lit up. 'Are you sure?' she said. She put the receiver down, and turned to Jenkins. 'Arrange for all of The Summerhouse Players to meet us at the Twixton Arts Theatre. We have an interesting development…'

The stage at the theatre was still decked out as a posh Edwardian dining room. As DCI Summersby stood, centre stage, it was a surreal sight to see each member of The Summerhouse Players, now dressed in their casual attire, sitting in the various leather armchairs and settees of the set. Jenkins and a police officer stood in attendance stage-left.

'Thank you all for attending at such short notice,' she said.

'Will this take long?' asked Laurence Bigley, somewhat irritated.

'As long as is necessary,' replied Summersby. 'As you all know,' she continued. 'Mister Harding was not the most popular member of The Summerhouse Players.'

'You *could* say that,' muttered Tim Quinton.

A muffled cacophony of opinions was expressed by many in the group.

'But he didn't deserve to die the way he did.' Summersby let the statement sink in before continuing. 'He was poisoned, not by his own hand, but by somebody who is sitting here now.'

'And how could you possibly know that?' exclaimed Walter Delaney.

'That's easy… Motive. For example, you, Mister Delaney, were owed money from the deceased.'

'So?'

'Some might consider that a motive. After all, money is in short supply when you are unemployed, despite your… buying and selling.'

Delaney shook his head. 'You people never let go, do you?'

'You are without doubt disreputable. But do I think you are capable of murder?' Summersby shook her head. 'No.' She looked at Ian King. Mister King, you described Mister Harding as a narcissist.'

'What of it? It was common knowledge that he only cared about himself.'

'His membership of a far-right political party suggests that he was also a racist.'

Ian looked disheartened. He hesitated before responding. 'I've experienced racism in many forms,' he said, sadly. 'Alex was very unpleasant in lots of ways, but I learned to deal with it in my own way.' He looked pleadingly at DCI Summersby. 'I'm not a killer.'

Summersby nodded her head sympathetically. She turned her attention to Tina Stapleton. 'When you were interviewed, Miss Stapleton, you failed to mention that you had a past history with the deceased?'

'I didn't think it relevant,' she said. 'Water under the bridge.'

'Alex Harding was a stage name, was it not?'

Tina fell silent for a long time before reluctantly responding. 'Yes.'

'His real name being Alex Pinkton.'

Debbie Pinkton turned to her mother. 'Mummy?'

Tina's eyes became watery. 'I'm sorry, Debbie.' She looked to DCI Summersby. 'Alex didn't want anything to do with my daughter, so I kept it quiet, and carried on as a single mother.'

'The deceased was behind in his child support, is that correct?'

'It's been a struggle, that's for sure.'

'Some might call that a motive,' suggested Summersby.

'You can call it what you want,' snapped Tina, defensively. 'I am not a murderer.'

Laurence Bigley decided to intervene. 'Leave her alone. Have a heart, Inspector. She didn't kill Alex.'

Summersby turned to Laurence. 'Ah. Mister Bigley. You sound very sure of yourself. Why is that I wonder?'

'I don't know what you're talking about. Really, I don't.'

Summersby now stood before Laurence. 'You said something in your interview that intrigued me at the time.'

'I don't recall what I said.'

'You said *What goes around…*'

'Figure of speech.'

'Alex Harding was poisoned with Quinticidal Ultra, Mister Bigley.'

'What of it?'

'You're a keen gardener, are you not? It's an insecticide, as you well know.'

Laurence looked angry. 'A lot of people are gardeners, Inspector.'

'Robert Panning committed suicide, didn't he Mister Bigley?'

Laurence became sullen. 'Yes...'

'You lived together, did you not? You were a couple.' Laurence's eyes became moist. 'It was your touch DNA on the bottle of apple juice that was tainted with poison... Mister Bigley, *you* killed Alex Harding.'

The rest of The Summerhouse Players stared at Laurence in disbelief.

Laurence looked to DCI Summersby, with a pained expression. 'Robert was my life. Alex's bullying of him was despicable. Beyond the pale. He as good as killed him. I had to have retribution. You must see that?'

'That, Mister Bigley, will be for the courts to decide. You are under arrest for the murder of Alex Harding. You do not have to say anything. But it may harm your defence if you do not mention when questioned something which you later rely on in court.' She summoned silently for Jenkins to escort Laurence Bigley to the police station.

Jenkins, accompanied by a police officer, handcuffed Laurence Bigley and took him away, stage-left.

DCI Summersby waited for a few minutes before finally addressing the rest of The Summerhouse Players. 'Thank you for your time and patience in this matter,' she said. 'It's always distressing in an investigation of this kind, to learn that somebody you knew was involved in the death of a colleague.' She began walking across the stage, briefly stopping as if an afterthought had suddenly occurred to her. She turned to The Summerhouse Players for one last time.

'You know, they say the show must go on. It would be a shame to let this affair be the end of the line.'

It was Albert who responded. 'You know,' he said. 'Once the dust has settled, I rather think the show *will* go on.'

DCI Summersby exited stage-left.

The Suitcase

Gerald Billingham shook the rainwater from his umbrella, before he entered his late father's small detached cottage. He was glad to be out of the autumnal wind and rain that had persisted throughout the day.

It was a remote property, situated in the heart of the New Forest in Hampshire, surrounded by trees and grassland, and had taken quite a time to locate in the drive over from London. He hadn't been here since he was a boy, as he was estranged from his father since his parents' divorce years ago. Now in his late-fifties, Gerald was the last of the Billinghams, after his mother's death roughly a decade ago.

He felt like he was stepping back in time as he looked around. An old clock sat on a mantelpiece, above an open fireplace, next to some framed photographs and a radio. There was an old settee against the far wall that had seen better days. In the middle of the room was a small wooden table with a couple of chairs. Various antique ornaments and books festooned a shelf unit far right beside a small window. A door to the left gave access to the kitchen, and a staircase to the right led to his father's bedroom.

Gerald put his wet umbrella in a nearby stand, took off his raincoat, and hung it up on a hook by the front door. There were low wooden beams in the cottage, and because he was quite tall, he felt slightly claustrophobic; it was good to get out of the wet and windy weather though, and he brushed his short brown hair back into position roughly with his hand. He decided to light a fire and placed several logs and coal from the hearth into the fireplace, along with some paper, and lit it with a match.

The fire made the cottage feel more homely, and Gerald began to feel less stressed than he had been of late. His father's funeral was a low-key affair, and only a few mourners were there to see him off.

As he stood before the fire, drying off his wet jeans, and warming himself up from the winter chill, he thought about his father, Eddie, and tried to conjure up some memories from his childhood, but they were few and far between.

The plain truth of the matter was that Eddie was a complete stranger to him.

Once Gerald was suitably dried off, he went into the kitchen in search of a warming drink. He found an unopened bottle of brandy and poured himself a generous amount of it into a glass; the fiery liquid warmed him a little as he took his first sip.

He decided to explore his father's old cottage...

Entering his father's bedroom, Gerald was immediately struck at how neat everything was. The bed had a folded blanket and duvet upon it, beside a feathered pillow. On a small table beside the bed was a book and a small table lamp; he picked up the book, which was titled The Murder On The Links, by Agatha Christie – Gerald noticed that it was a library book, and had missed its return date by several months. He replaced the book, and made a mental note to return it to the library when he had the chance.

An old wardrobe contained his father's few clothes. Not much to show for a man who was in his late-seventies, he thought, sadly. There were a couple of dark suits, some shirts, ties, trousers, and an array of pullovers neatly folded on a shelf. At the base of the wardrobe were some black shoes, impressively polished and shined. If anything, thought Gerald, Eddie was fastidiously tidy – much more so than *he* ever was, he concluded.

As he looked around the room, at various pictures on the walls, something caught his eye. Under Eddie's bed was a small black leather suitcase; Gerald put his glass down upon the table, pulled the suitcase out, placed it on the bed, and then he sat beside it. It was a very old suitcase which was surprisingly heavy, and a lot of the leather was peeling off. What if it was locked, he thought? He felt strangely guilty - as if he was intruding upon his father's privacy. It was probably full of old papers and nothing of any note, he surmised. He hesitated before successfully opening the clasps. He lifted the lid of the suitcase, and saw that inside it were various old photographs, an assortment of letters still in their envelopes, as well as an abundance of utility bills.

He closed the suitcase, and, glass in hand, took it downstairs.

He laid the suitcase on the small wooden table in the centre of the room, sat down, and opened it again. Rummaging through the photographs, Gerald could see that many of the black and white images were of his father when he was a young man. One of the pictures was of Eddie beside his motorbike. To see his father as a virile young man, back in the day, was both a revelation and a welcome surprise. There were several photographs of Eddie and Gerald's late mother Irene. He could see that his mother was very beautiful when she was a young woman. They were clearly in love at the time, and their pictures must have been taken perhaps just before they became engaged and later married. He suddenly felt a sense of melancholy as he continued to look at the images that had taken him to a moment in time that had remained hidden and forgotten for so many years.

As Gerald continued looking at the photographs, there was one that drew his attention; it was of his father beside another young man – they were in front of their motorbikes, and were clearly the best of friends. The other young man looked vaguely familiar, but Gerald thought little of it at the time. He turned the photograph over in his hand; there was an inscription on the back: *E and Joe Foster, Isle of Man.*

The rain outside began to deteriorate, and occasional flashes of lightning now encroached the room through the thin curtains. Despite the worsening weather, Gerald felt safe and comfortable in the cottage, as he took further sips from his brandy, and continued exploring the contents of the suitcase.

Seeing his father as a young man changed Gerald's perspective of him. He had no recollection of him other than as a stranger who left his life when he was a young boy. Why did he leave? What was the catalyst that sparked his exodus? Gerald suddenly felt the urge to get to the bottom of this enigmatic man. Who *was* he? What was his story? Gerald instinctively felt that the answers to these questions were somehow within this dilapidated old suitcase that had remained hidden for so many years.

There were many pictures of his father and mother, newly married, outside of a church. Beside them were various other members of the family as well as Joe Foster, who Gerald presumed was Eddie's best man at the time. Everybody looked so happy. What went wrong? Why did they end up divorced? Nobody had ever bothered to give him a clear reason.

As he continued to leaf through the photographs, he came across one of his father wearing a military uniform. Perhaps that is why he couldn't remember much about him? Maybe he served overseas? On the back of the photograph was written *E beginning national service taken by JF*. Joe Foster was clearly Eddie's close friend. Gerald was glad that his father had a friend during the time of the cold war; he would have served two years away from home. Away from Irene… He wondered if Joe had also served national service, after all they seemed about the same age.

There was a photograph that showed Eddie and Joe in a dark lounge of a house somewhere; Eddie was in uniform, but Joe was not. On the back of the photograph was written *E and JF at JF's house 46 Limbard Street, London.*

Gerald decided to look through some of the many letters that were still in their opened envelopes. Perhaps they would give a greater insight into his father, he thought. As he read one of the letters, he felt as though he was intruding upon a time long ago that was perhaps best left alone, but the pull of his curiosity had the better of him, and he began to read:

Dear Eddie,
I miss you more than words can say. I love being Mrs Billingham and keep looking at my wedding ring to make sure I'm not dreaming! It's so cruel that you are there and I am here. It's not fair. I'm sure that two years isn't forever though and I look forward to the time when we can be together again and for the rest of our lives.
Sleep tight.
Lots of love,
Irene x

Gerald felt the weight of heartbreak his parents must have felt during that time of his father's absence. It was an uncertain time in the world. His mother was right – it wasn't fair. They were newlyweds, and circumstances dictated that they were to be apart for two years. Two long years... Shortly after the second world war, Russia had become a potential enemy, despite being allies during the war, and now they had nuclear weapons, and were considered a danger to the western world. Conscription of young men followed until the early nineteen-sixties.

He replaced the letter to its envelope, and picked up another...

Dear Eddie,

Joe paid a visit the other day. He sends his regards and wishes he could have enlisted with you. His flat feet say otherwise!

My daily routine has become something of a drudge. With money being short it's hard to find food that doesn't cost an arm and a leg. Your mother has been very supportive and I know that we are lucky that she has a spare room for us. It will be nice when we can get our own little nest in the future.

Sleep tight.
Lots of love,
Irene x

With a heavy heart, Gerald continued to browse through the many letters of correspondence that must have been received by his father while he was stationed overseas, in Germany, during his enforced conscription. Most of the letters from Irene were of similar content, but the next one he read came as something of an unexpected shock.

Dear Eddie,

There is no easy way for me to tell you this but I am pregnant. I was so lonely and depressed during your absence. I know this is no excuse and I wouldn't blame you if you wanted nothing more to do with me. It was a moment of weakness with Joe. He feels as bad as I do and we've promised not to see each other ever again. I don't know what to do. I'm at such a weak point in my life and have to consider all options. I'm worried that your mother will soon find out and will no longer want me living here. I'm so sorry to be giving you such bad news and if I could turn back the

clock things would be different. I know you won't believe this but I still love you.
Irene x

Holy shit.

Gerald stared at the letter, momentarily dumbfounded. The shock of its contents was palpable. This changes everything, he thought. The man he thought was his father was his father's best friend. Talk about betrayal... He downed the remains of his brandy, but it didn't seem to calm his nerves – if anything it only magnified the hurt that he felt inside. He wasn't sure who he felt sorry for – his mother or his father? He felt conflicted. Cruel circumstances had separated them at a time when they needed each other more than ever.

He knew that his parents divorced when he was a small boy, so his father must have tried to make the best of a bad situation for a few years until the marriage naturally dissolved.

He retrieved the brandy bottle, and filled his glass. He sat on the settee, mulling things over in his head. He had a biological father who he knew nothing about. Eddie had given him a start in life and tried to do the right thing, but in the end, it must have been too much for him.

As he sat drinking the rest of his brandy, the weight of the revelation began to lighten as his eyes began to feel heavy. He resolved to find out more about Joe Foster the next day. What became of him? Is he even still alive? Does he even know that I exist, he wondered?

He fell into a deep sleep...

A few days later, Gerald was back in his flat in Lambeth, South London. With the scant information he had about Joe Foster, Gerald used social media and public records to try and locate his biological father; he had an old address and a name. He could roughly guess Joe's age. Sadly, there were scores of Joe Fosters and it seemed that Gerald had reached a dead end.

It was then that he decided to contact a third party to do the work on his behalf. He saw an ad online for a company called Let Us Find Your Relative. It wasn't cheap, but Gerald felt that it would be money well spent if it meant learning more about Joe. He contacted them with the few details that he had, paid the fee, and waited for them to respond.

Several days went by, and Gerald began thinking that his efforts were in vain. It was then that he noticed a new email on his laptop.

They found him...

His full name was Joseph Reginald Foster, and he was aged seventy-eight; he lived at 23 Hashington Lane, Bethnal Green, East London.

Gerald was filled with mixed emotions. A lot of water had passed under the bridge, and he wondered if meeting Joe, and declaring himself as his son, was the right thing to do; after all, the shock might be too much for an elderly man who had lived his entire life possibly not knowing that he even *existed*. How would he react? Would he even acknowledge Gerald?

A few days passed before he finally summoned up the courage to visit Joe.

As he was driving in his car, Gerald thought back to when he was a boy, more than fifty years ago. His mother, Irene, struggled as a single mum with little money coming in. He assumed that Eddie had paid some money to her in child support, but it probably wasn't much, as she had to do a part-time cleaning job to keep a roof over their heads.

He recalled hearing her crying at night. This would be a regular feature of his formative years. It must have been a tough time for her trying to make ends meet. Back then there would have been a stigma to being a single parent. Others in the community would have made her feel shame. Perhaps she experienced knowing glances from other married women, who would have looked down upon her from their elevated status.

As the passing houses became just a blur, he opened the car window fully on the driver side, and tried to clear his head, but despite the cold air now felt against his face, images and conversations, once lost, now filled his mind. He could see his mother looking out of the window of their flat, tea in hand, perhaps thinking of what could have been.

She never remarried…

As he approached Hashington Lane, Gerald felt a sense of foreboding. It would be like travelling in time; after all, the only time he had seen Joe was in an old photograph, from when he was a young man. People change… sometimes beyond belief.

He found number 23, parked the car outside, and got out. As he approached the narrow terraced house, Gerald was struck by how unprepossessing it looked. The small front garden was overgrown with weeds, and the front of the property had been infested with ivy upon its wall.

He rang the doorbell.

He could hear footsteps slowly approaching. The door opened, and standing before Gerald was an old man, dressed in a white shirt, long grey cardigan, black trousers, and slippers. Although he was seventy-eight years of age, he retained a full head of grey hair. Gerald could see a vague but discernible resemblance to the photographs of the young man he had found in his late father's suitcase, and he suddenly felt a sense of melancholy unexpectedly come over him.

Beside Joe's feet was a small, scruffy, black-haired mongrel dog; they both looked to Gerald as though he was from another planet. Joe was clearly not used to anyone intruding upon his private domain.

'Yes?' he asked, weakly.

Gerald offered his hand. 'I'm Gerald Billingham. I believe you knew my late father, Eddie?'

Joe shook Gerald's hand, instinctively, but seemed confused.

'Eddie?' he replied, uncertainly.

Gerald took out a photograph of both his late father and Joe, taken in the Isle of Man, beside their motorbikes, and showed it to him. 'Perhaps this will jog your memory?' he said.

As Joe took the photograph and looked at it, his eyes became misty. He looked at Gerald, and smiled briefly. 'You'd best come in,' he said, warmly.

Gerald found himself in a dimly-lit dining room. It was an unkempt space, with old newspapers strewn here and there on an old worn carpet. Unlike Eddie, Joe was an untidy man.

Gerald sat by a table, while Joe sat in his armchair; Joe's dog faithfully lay down beside his master's feet.

'Please excuse the mess,' said Joe. 'I keep meaning to smarten the place up, but for some reason I never get round to it.'

'Perfectly okay,' said Gerald. 'I'm much the same.'

'I was expecting my daughter. She'll be round any minute now.' Joe looked at the photograph still in his hand, and studied it. 'God... Is that really me?'

'You and Eddie were both bikers?'

Joe nodded. 'It was back in the day when you could get away with doing a ton down a motorway. Didn't even wear helmets, half the time.'

'You were good friends back then?'

Joe looked at the photograph once more, and nodded. 'Oh yes,' he said. 'We were.' There was a wistful expression in his eyes. 'Time goes by so quickly, doesn't it?'

There was something in Joe's demeanour that Gerald found appealing. Perhaps it was a shared view of the world, he wondered, or a genetic connection that he instinctively felt for this frail, elderly man before him. 'What do you remember about Eddie?' he asked.

Joe thought long and hard before responding. 'It was such a long time ago,' he said. 'We lost touch... I suppose these things happen, don't they? After he did his national service, I didn't hear from him again.'

Gerald could detect a sense of regret in Joe's tone. Has he put everything in the past and simply moved on, he wondered? After all, they were the best of friends. Losing your best friend because of a foolish mistake must have been traumatic for him as well as Eddie. Gerald didn't want to open up a Pandora's box, but he had to know more... 'What do you remember about Irene?' he asked.

Joe looked at Gerald for the longest time. His expression was one of shock and sadness; he was just about to reply when the front doorbell rang. 'That will be my daughter,' he said, finally, and went to open the door.

When the door was opened there was a lady, probably in her early-thirties, dressed in a nurse's uniform, and she was holding a small black bag.

'Hello, Mister Foster. How are you today?' she said.

'Julie. Come in.' Joe let the nurse in, and closed the door.

'It's still Rosemary, but that's okay,' she said. She glanced briefly at Gerald. 'Oh, you have a guest. I can come by later if you'd like?'

Joe looked at Gerald, with some consternation. 'This is…'

'Gerald.' Gerald offered his hand to the nurse, and she shook it. 'Mister Foster knew my late father, in his youth.'

'Pleased to meet you,' she said.

'Gerald was showing me a photograph of when I was young,' said Joe, and he showed the photograph to Rosemary.

'You were a handsome chap, Mister Foster,' she replied. She then turned to Gerald, and spoke in a quiet tone. 'It's really therapeutic for our clients like Mister Foster to look back on their lives. It will often spur a memory, which is important, given their condition.' She turned back to Joe, who was now seated. 'Have you had your lunch yet?' she asked.

'Oh yes,' he replied.

Rosemary stroked the dog. 'And how about this fellow? Has he been fed?'

'Oh err…'

It dawned on Gerald that Joe was not a well man, and his *condition* was sadly quite common for people of a certain vintage. He felt that he didn't want to intrude on Joe anymore, so he gave his excuses and left, promising to look in on him every so often.

As he was driving on his return journey, Gerald made himself a pledge to get to know Joe more, and visit him as often as he could, while there was still time. He opened the car window on the driver's side fully, and let the air cool his face. Life was strange, he thought. If it wasn't for that old suitcase he would never have known of his real father's existence. We are all human, he concluded, and we all have our faults and weaknesses. He could tell that Joe was a kind man. A gentle man.

The tears that suddenly fell cascaded down his cheeks.

The Bookworm and The Ghosts

It was the day that George Entwerp had dreaded for so many years... the final day of trading in his shop, Entwerp's Classic Books Emporium. He had owned the shop for over thirty years, which was about half of his life, and now he found himself forced to close it because people were mostly buying books online, and the increased market in ebooks had meant that his books weren't selling as well as they once did. In fact, days would go by, and he would be lucky to even make a single sale. True to say, he was not a particularly astute businessman, and he hadn't moved with the times, and now was paying the ultimate price.

The rates for the property, and the overheads, had gone up significantly over the last couple of years, and he was in danger of going under if he continued trading. George lived by himself above the shop, in a small but comfortable flat.

Today he was selling most of his books for less than half price, and many people had come into his shop, and bagged a bargain.

George was a man of insignificant stature. He was neither tall nor short, handsome nor ugly, fat nor thin. His was a face that easily melted into the crowd, but he was an intelligent and honest man whose love of literature was beyond measure. He was a confirmed bachelor. Some might conjecture that he was married to his books.

The building, on the outskirts of West London, was first built in the mid-Victorian period, and, despite minor alterations, it had maintained that sense of architectural integrity and refinement that the Victorians seemed to value so much. There were shelves with books that lined every wall, and a row of aisles in between shelf units with books at the far end of the shop. Each book was carefully positioned in alphabetical order of their respective authors. A small table, with seats, was in the middle of the shop, for those customers who liked to sit and read before purchasing a book.

He had probably read most of the books that were on the shelves, and he prided himself that he also knew about the lives of many of the authors. To George, these were not just books, they were a moment in time captured in print.

The bookshop had been up for sale over the last few months, and he had had an offer from a prospective buyer who wanted to turn the premises into a dental practice. Once the sale was complete, George decided, he would buy a small dwelling by the sea, perhaps Brighton, and live out his life reading his beloved books.

Suffice to say, George was a bookworm.

As the last customer had now left the premises, George went about his customary practice of closing and locking the door, changing the sign to CLOSED, taking the receipts from the till, and balancing the books. He did this as he had done for over thirty years, almost instinctively, but as he was writing the last entry in his accounts ledger, it suddenly dawned on him that this would be the last entry before enforced retirement, and the impact of it now weighed heavily on his shoulders. Over thirty years… He was a relatively young man when he first opened Entwerp's Classic Books Emporium, and he recalled the pride and excitement that he had felt in those early years. It was at a time when people still read books. It was difficult for George to comprehend why people weren't as in love with books as he was. Just the feel of a book in your hand, even the smell of it… was intoxicating.

His love of books began from an early age when he first read The Adventures of Huckleberry Finn. The book captured his attention and drew him down a path that he felt compelled to follow. Like Lewis Carroll's Alice, he followed the eponymous white rabbit to a place of wonderment... a world where he could escape the drudgery of his parent's incessant marital disharmony. It was a place of refuge for a boy with unlimited imagination.

George unlocked the door that led to the stairway, and he then walked up to his flat. It felt like a long day, and he was tired and needed some rest, but first he would make himself some dinner and then read for a while before retiring for the evening. His was a solitary existence, but he had become accustomed to his own company. He was a loner since his youth, and had always found it difficult to make meaningful relationships with others. He felt a kinship with books more than he did people, and this trend continued into adulthood.

The flat was mostly open-planned. There was a carpeted living area that had a long settee, a table and chairs, and a small television on a stand. George's bed was on a raised area in the corner of the room. Through a door was a small but well-maintained kitchen. Through another door was the bathroom. The ceiling throughout was high, as with a lot of Victorian properties, and still had the original ornate cornices at its edges. Picture rails still adorned each wall, in keeping with period values. Although the furnishings were modern, the flat maintained the feel of a mid-nineteenth century house. It was dimly-lit and had an aura that George felt at home with.

George cooked himself an omelette, and sat down on the settee to eat it; after he had finished, he made himself a hot drink and watched some news on television. His mind drifted to the events of the day, and he found himself immersed in negative thoughts. How sad that it had come to this, he reasoned. How would he adapt to a different way of life?

As the evening wore on, and the darkness of night deepened, George took a hot shower, changed into his pyjamas, and went to bed. He left a small light on beside the bed, picked up a book that he had left beside the pillow, and began reading; it was a biography of Agatha Christie, and it was a voluminous book.

Having read for a couple of hours, George noticed the light begin to slowly flicker. He put the book down, and checked that the lightbulb was firmly in place. Perhaps the bulb was on its last legs, he thought.

The light went out, and the room was suddenly left in near pitch-darkness. George got up from the bed, put on his dressing gown and slippers, and made his way to the main light switch. Having fumbled for the switch, he pressed it down but nothing happened. It must be the fuse, he decided. The fuse box was situated in the shop below; he would have to go downstairs and check it. He managed to extract a small torch from a drawer in the kitchen, switched it on, and made his way to the stairway.

As George was walking down the steps, he noticed that there was a sharp drop in temperature, and he could now see wisps of vapour emanating from his mouth and nose as he exhaled. He turned the collar of his dressing gown up around his neck to protect against the harsh chill. The cold air gave him goosebumps as he entered the shop. For good measure he flipped the light switch but nothing happened.

George located the fuse box, which was at the far end of the first aisle, at the base of the wall. He opened up the fuse box but nothing seemed untoward… the fuses had not been tripped and he could see no reason for the loss of electricity… it was then that he heard something nearby which startled him: it was the sound of somebody breathing, besides himself. 'Is anyone there?' he called out, in a voice that feigned courage but betrayed fear. A long silence elapsed. The response that he heard was barely a whisper, but it was real nonetheless.

'Yes.'

George felt the hairs on the back of his neck stand up. He had never felt fear of this magnitude. His hand trembled as he directed the small torch about him. The voice seemed to come from one of the other aisles. 'I've got a weapon…' he declared, 'and I'm not afraid to use it.' He went to the next aisle, and shined his torch down it, but there was nothing there. Could it have been my imagination, he wondered; after all, it's been known for the mind to concoct all sorts of illusions under stress, and he had been under an awful lot of it lately.

Just as he was about to remove himself from the shop, and return to his flat, something inexplicably caught his eye… there was a faint but distinct glow coming from the next aisle. George felt his heart racing as he anxiously looked down the aisle, not knowing what to expect. He surreptitiously raised his torch, and pointed it towards the mysterious glow. What he saw momentarily took his breath away. He could discern a translucent apparition of a man, and he was reviewing the books on the shelf; he was dressed in a shabby white suit, buttoned white shirt, and matching shoes; his voluminous white hair, generous moustache and aquiline features were instantly familiar to George. It was unmistakeable. But surely, it couldn't be, could it? This was ridiculous. When the apparition turned to George, and spoke in his mild South American drawl, it nailed it:

'You have a fine collection of books, George, and that's a fact.'

It was such a moment of surreal incredulity that George didn't know whether to run, whether to scream, or whether to respond... for some unaccountable reason, only known to himself, he chose the latter: 'Thank you,' he said, somewhat hesitantly, trembling in fright.

The unequivocal figure of Mark Twain, holding a book, turned towards George, and proceeded to walk slowly through him, as though he wasn't even there, into the centre of the shop where he calmly sat down at the coffee table. 'Let's talk awhile,' he said, and put the book down on the table in front of him.

Although George was temporarily rooted to the spot in fear, there was something about this ghostly figure that intrigued him; after all, this was his favourite author from when he was knee-high, and the opportunity to talk openly with his spiritual hero far outweighed the human frailties that he was doubtlessly now experiencing. Although a bundle of nerves, George somehow summoned the courage, from somewhere deep inside, and sat down at the coffee table, opposite Twain. He didn't know what to say... what *could* you say to a corpse that happens to be sitting opposite you? He could comment that he was looking remarkably well, considering that he had been *dead* for over a hundred years. Perhaps he should make small talk... the weather was always a hot topic of conversation in England... No... This was an opportunity, unlike any other, to connect with his lifelong hero, and he would be a fool not to take advantage of the opportunity, no matter how daunting the task might be. But what could he say to someone considered a consummate wit, deep-thinker and raconteur, as well as one of America's giants in literature? Given the circumstance that he found himself in, George simply said: 'I've been an admirer of your work ever since I was a boy.'

Twain looked George in the eye, and there was an understanding, a link of sorts that he had not experienced, *ever*, with another human being, albeit one that had ceased living long ago. 'I know,' he replied, simply. There was a tinge of melancholy in his tone. 'You have an uncommon propensity for literature, George, and that's a fact. We select few are beholden to your interest in our works, for sure. Why, your enthusiasm for the written word helps keep our memory alive.'

George was taken aback. This spiritual presence that glowed before him spoke with eloquence and undoubted earnestness. There were so many questions he wanted to ask him, but was unsure, given the unusual situation he found himself in, whether it was the right thing to do. After all, he did not know the social etiquette involved when communicating with a ghost. 'How do you know my name?' he asked.

'There are more mysteries in this existence than you can shake a stick at, and if I had a nickel for each of 'em I'd be a mighty rich man.'

Twain's humorous articulation made George feel less inhibited than before, and he wanted to make the most of this opportunity. He no longer felt afraid. In fact, he felt invigorated. Rejuvenated. How many people get to meet their heroes, he wondered, even though his hero happened to have been long-since departed, and pushing up the daisies.

George pinched himself hard to test whether he was dreaming. It *hurt*. He *wasn't* dreaming. No. Perhaps he was having a psychotic attack? After all, he had been under a *lot* of stress lately, what with the bookshop and its imminent collapse. As he looked at the spectral figure seated opposite him, the clarity of his features, the chilled air undoubtedly emanating from his very being, George concluded that this was all real. Besides… there were so many things in life, as in death, that were still unaccountable and unexplained: sightings of UFOs, Bigfoot, ghosts, objects moving by themselves, people dying from spontaneous combustion, as well as other countless phenomena. Why *shouldn't* it be real, he reasoned?

But what to say to an Icon of literature? George thought back to some of the books that he had read by Mark Twain: Adventures of Huckleberry Finn; The Adventures of Tom Sawyer; The Mysterious Stranger to name but a few. Perhaps he could ask: *Where did you draw inspiration for your novels*? But George already knew the answer to that: from Twain's own experience growing up and into early adulthood.

Instead, George simply asked: 'What is it like? I mean, being…'

'Deceased?' Twain responded. 'Of course, I would have preferred the alternative, but given the circumstance it's an acceptable way of life. I come and go as I please. I don't need to be fed or watered, and best of all I don't pay taxes.'

George laughed like he had never laughed before. Mark Twain was *the* perfect unexpected dead guest that he could have envisaged.

There was one question that George felt compelled to ask: 'Earlier, you said: *We select few*. What did you mean?'

'Darn it. I'd forget my britches if they weren't already on. Where are my manners? Let me introduce you to my esteemed colleagues,' he said, and turned towards the aisles.

Eerie glows began gradually materialising from aisles two and four. George felt an increased chill in the room, and the hairs on the back of his neck stood up in expectation and shock.

The first spirit to slowly emerge from aisle two was an elderly, elegant-looking, gentleman wearing a vivid green velvet jacket with yellow waistcoat, white shirt, a broad velvet blue bow tie, brown trousers, and patent leather shoes. He had a fine long grey beard, high forehead, and a thinning head of curly grey hair carefully combed over from the side. He had large dark expressive eyes that emitted kindness and empathy. George immediately recognised him as the author of books such as: Oliver Twist, Bleak House, and David Copperfield.

The second spirit to slowly emerge from aisle four was that of a slim woman in her late fifties, wearing a long black dress, matching shoes, pearl necklace and a long dark coat with fur lapels. Her face had sharp features with intelligent, but sad, brown eyes. Her long auburn hair was tied up in a bun at the back. George immediately recognised her as the author of such books as: A Room of One's Own, To The Lighthouse, and Orlando.

Charles Dickens, ever the gentleman, took Virginia Woolf's hand, and escorted her to the table. Woolf sat next to Twain's left, with Dickens to his right.

George was in seventh heaven. He was now sitting with three of his favourite authors of all time. It was literally an out-of-this-world experience that he didn't want to ever end. Of course, he knew that each of the three spirits had certainly had their faults when they were alive and kicking: Mark Twain was notoriously cantankerous, and had a fondness for strong liquor; Charles Dickens was a known philanderer, and treated his long-suffering wife appallingly; Virginia Woolf had a complicated love life because of her bisexuality, which was misunderstood between the two World Wars – she suffered with metal anguish throughout her life, and tragically committed suicide by drowning at a relatively young age.

Each of them had their human weaknesses, and that was what made them so appealing to George, because, despite their many idiosyncrasies, they still managed to write some of the greatest novels he had ever read, which, in his eyes, secured their status as legends in the pantheon of world literature.

'May I say, Mister Entwerp-' began Dickens.
'Please… call me George.'

'*George…* that it is with immense humility that we find ourselves in your company, at a time of great personal upheaval for you. You have been unerringly supportive of our efforts, and for that we are here to express our eternal gratitude.'

Woolf nodded her assent.

'Thank *you*,' replied George, in earnest.

'You have dedicated your life to the written word,' said Woolf. 'As have we. It is because of your intense devotion, knowledge and enthusiasm for our work, that we are compelled to join you for this moment in time.'

'But how is that possible?' asked George, in stunned disbelief.

'It is not of our making,' replied Woolf. 'It is from a force far greater than our own. The mysteries in life, as in death, are multitudinous in number, as you will one day come to realise.'

Only Virginia Woolf would use such a word as *multitudinous*, thought George. But if she was right, and George had no reason to doubt her, given the circumstances, then anything is possible, and that thought gave him comfort in his time of need, and for the long road ahead.

Just to be in the company of his heroes gave George food for thought. 'What was it that motivated all of you to write novels?' he asked, generally.

Dickens was the first to respond, after a moment's hesitation. 'As well as my indulgence in the dramatic arts, I found that I also had an innate capacity for storytelling, and conveying such in the accumulation of the written word that spoke to the hearts and minds of everyday people. By appealing to the populace, I achieved more than I ever could have imagined, and maintained a standard of work that kept me far from the workhouse.' As an afterthought, he added: 'Contrary to my father, I recognised the need for diligent labour and its economic necessity.'

George knew from his reading of Dickens' life that his father, John Dickens, was a source of some anxiety for him when he was younger. His father, suffice to say, despite having a good job with the Navy Pay Office, was not efficient with money and, because of debts accrued, was arrested and imprisoned in Marshalsea Prison – Charles was twelve years old at the time, and had to work up to ten hours a day in Warren's Blacking Factory, fixing labels to jars of boot polish, in order to bring some money into the household. Up until his father's death, at the age of sixty-six, Dickens had financially supported him throughout, and kept him at bay from his many creditors.

'For me,' said Twain, 'the key to the longevity in my writing came about because of my natural affinity for words, from the time when I worked as a printer's apprentice at the tender age of thirteen. With persistence of endeavour, and the wonderment of imagination, I strived to maintain an honesty and integrity in my stories that appealed to the working masses and beyond. What motivated me was seeing my work in print, and putting food on the table. Simple as that. Hell, there's no quick secret to success of any kind – half the time it's just getting started. I would say that it's no different to somebody who is skilled at baking a cake. As long as you have all the ingredients, it's just a matter of coordination and expedience. Suffice to say… I've burned a few cakes in my time.' He laughed richly at his own humour, and Dickens instinctively joined in, with Woolf smiling fondly.

To hear the wisdom of Twain, from his own lips, was beyond measure for George. It was simplistic but real – a true testament of endeavour that explained his creative process and his endurance as a giant in the field of literature.

'For my small part in all of this,' said Woolf, 'I was fortunate that my affluent parents had a full library of books, and I read voraciously as many books as I could, when I was a young girl. It was a healthy distraction from the very unhealthy attention I was subjected to by my two older half-brothers. It was a juxtaposition of joy and evil that I had to contend with for the rest of my life. Writing a diary from an early age helped me to live with the depression and anxiety that plagued me from time to time.'

Dickens shook his head, sadly. 'Madam, your plight has been one that you have had to contend with for the longest time. I commend you for your strength of purpose and humanity.'

Twain nodded his agreement. 'Your ability to rise above such disagreeable experience is to your undying credit.'

Woolf smiled faintly, but it was a sad, almost indifferent smile that conveyed a life torn by mental anguish, culminating in her death by her own volition. 'Without the benefit of my writing,' she said, 'I would have simply perished far sooner than I did; you see... it provided me with the fortitude to live with my demons until the moment when I could cope no more. You might say that it was a crutch that sustained me in my hour of need... albeit temporarily...'

George was struck by how touchingly *English* Woolf's words were; they were full of matter-of-fact pathos; full of reserve that the English were particularly renowned for, and to some extent still are. But within those telling words was a dark recess of the human condition. Despite overwhelming odds, she, like Dickens and Twain, rose above obstacles that were placed in their way, to become literary giants. Their spirit exemplified human endeavour at its best.

As George looked upon the three spirits before him, their glow now slowly fading into obscurity, he discovered within himself a new, powerful, feeling of optimism that he hadn't felt for the longest time. Despite his own personal dilemma, he instinctively knew that all would be well –

after all, his own problems were in the material world; there was a *spiritual* world that was beyond the human experience. As long as he maintained his love for books, and their authors, his life would not be a wasted one.

Now sitting at the table, conspicuously alone, George's own spirit was elevated by his encounter with his three literary heroes. As he sat in happy contemplation, he noticed the book that lay on the table in front of him: it was the Adventures of Huckleberry Finn. He picked up the book, and opened it. Inside, on the title page was an inscription, and it read:

To George
Life, as in death, is mighty mysterious.
Keep the faith!
Your old pal, S.L. Clemens
(Mark Twain)

Eleanor Finally Meets Her Match

Eleanor Devington still missed her husband with a passion. She was seventy-two years of age, and had been a widow for well over ten years, and yet the sorrow she felt was no different now to what it was then. She loved her husband, and each new day she would merrily say: *'Good morning, Charlie,'* to the urn that sat on the mantlepiece, above the fireplace, that contained his ashes... as if he was still very much alive.

Charlie had died suddenly from a heart attack, brought on by gastroenteritis, leaving her all alone in the world. Towards the end of his life, he had suffered with stomach cramps, and in the end the strain was too much for him. The coroner was very understanding, and conveyed his heartfelt sympathies to Eleanor, who was very appreciative.

Eleanor knew that she was at the tail-end of her life, and so she decided to enjoy it while she still could; besides... the insurance payout from Charlie's life insurance was enough to buy a fancy house in Eastbourne with all the trimmings, so why shouldn't she? Still sprightly, despite the odd twinge of rheumatism, and - despite her now-silver hair - she had maintained her relatively youthful appearance. Standing at five foot seven inches in her stockinged feet, she hadn't succumbed to shrinkage like a lot of her contemporaries. Wearing her favourite grey tweed skirt, white satin blouse with pearl necklace, silk nylons and stylish black suede shoes, Eleanor was every inch that of a merry widow. She enjoyed the small luxuries that money provided, such as a nice house by the sea, a shiny new car in her garage, elegant clothes, elegant jewellery, trips abroad, and money in the bank for essentials such as caviar, Chanel perfumes, and the odd cosmetic tuck here and there.

True to say, Charlie's demise allowed Eleanor to live the sort of life that she had often dreamed of ever since she was a young girl, but she missed the company of a man; she missed the company of a *husband*. Oh, she had had quite a few suitors over the years, since her husband's departure, but they were not really marriage material, but now she had her eye on a man who was just right: Dudley Solomon. He was balding, short, and slightly overweight, but he still had his own teeth. Although he occasionally suffered from mild angina, he was still in relatively good health. He was slightly older than Eleanor, but most of all… he was *rich*. Dudley was the owner of a chain of fish and chip shops in the area. He had a nice house, car, and money in the bank; he also had no dependants. He was thinking of retiring in the not-too-distant future. Perfect. They had met on a dating site called Twilight Romantics Dating Agency, which catered specifically for those of a certain vintage. Each had requested a soulmate who was kind, considerate, affable, and of independent means. Dudley was also a widower, so they had a lot in common. It was a match made in heaven, albeit via the internet.

Eleanor and Dudley met on numerous dates, such as eating at expensive restaurants, attending theatres where they would see the latest shows, and long weekends spent abroad. It was apparent that they clicked in a way that was conducive to them both; after all, they enjoyed the finer things in life, and each was looking for a permanent partner.

It was while they were busily tucking into frogs' legs, down the Champs-Élysées in Paris, that Dudley suddenly, and carefully, went down on one knee, and offered Eleanor his hand in marriage. The enormous sparkler that he presented to her glistened sufficiently enough for Eleanor to gleefully say: 'Yes.'

After they embraced in celebration, she almost snatched the ring out of his hand, and then sat for quite some time admiring the ornament that now proudly adorned her ring finger.

It sealed the deal.

After a short engagement, Eleanor and Dudley were married at the local registry office. It was a small ceremony with just a couple of witnesses in attendance.

Eleanor persuaded Dudley to sell his house – that way they could use her house for their newly-wedded life together; she also persuaded him to sell up his business, which meant that he could happily retire and enjoy travel and creature comforts with his new wife. Of course, she said, it made sense that they both made wills and took out life insurance policies; after all, they were not getting any younger...

Two years of wedded bliss had elapsed, when cracks began to appear in the seemingly idyllic union of Eleanor and Dudley. It all came to a sorry head on a Sunday morning, while Dudley was sat at the dining table tucking into his usual bowl of cornflakes. Eleanor, tea in hand, entered the room. 'Good morning, Charlie,' she said to her ex-husband, who as always was sitting on the mantlepiece, minding his own business. As an afterthought she then said: 'Dudley.'

'Ellie, isn't it time to say goodbye to Charlie?'

'Oh... I couldn't do *that* dear,' she replied, innocently.

'Why not?'

Eleanor looked to Dudley as though he had said something inconceivable. 'Because he was my husband, silly.'

Dudley was so incensed, that he nearly choked on his spoon. 'But *I'm* your husband.'

'Yes, but Charlie was my *first* husband,' she said, as though it made perfect sense in the grand scheme of things. She sat down at the table, opposite Dudley, calmly sipped from her delicate bone china cup of Earl Grey, and listened to her favourite soap The Archers on Radio Four.

Dudley was less than impressed that he had been surreptitiously relegated to husband number two. It suddenly dawned on him that, after all this time, they had run out of things to say to each other.

It occurred to Eleanor that being married to Dudley had become rather stale. They had travelled the globe together, enjoyed the luxuries that life had to offer a couple with inordinate wealth, but now… she was bored.

A silence of epic proportion entered the world of Eleanor and Dudley, and it wasn't about to go away.

Something had to give.

It was a lovely, warm, summer's day. The flowers were in full bloom, and the sun shone gloriously in a clear-blue sky. Eleanor wore a smart, expensive, long black silk dress. A gold brooch of an angel playing a harp adorned her cosmetically elevated chest. A stylish wide-brimmed black hat sat upon her carefully coiffured hair, and a pair of shiny black high-heeled shoes complimented her immaculately pedicured feet. She looked every inch the grieving widow as she got out of the limousine, and entered the crematorium.

There were only a handful of people in the congregation to see Dudley off; he had very few family members in attendance, and some of the workers from the fish and chip shops that he once owned, turned up to pay their respects. It was a short ceremony, and the official gave a lovely sermon which Eleanor found quite moving.

As Eleanor sat in the limousine returning her to her home, she thought back to what the coroner had said. He had concluded that Dudley's demise was due to his own negligence; after all, accidentally leaving the gas on unattended whilst having a catnap – one from which he never awoke – was never a good idea. He offered her his heartfelt condolences for her sad loss, and Eleanor was, once again, very appreciative.

Once more, Eleanor found herself living all alone, which of course was not entirely the case as she now had Dudley's remains, in an urn, beside that of Charlie's sitting proudly on the mantlepiece, to remind her of what once was. Some might think this rather unusual, but Eleanor had a veneer of steel; besides, she surmised, in her skewed logic, she saw their presence as proof of her undying love that she once shared with her late husbands. Each morning, when she entered her dining room, she would always greet her husbands with: 'Good morning, Charlie. Good morning, Dudley.' Occasionally she would even add, ironically: 'How are you today?' but their inevitable deathly silence spoke more than words ever could.

Although she was a widow once more, her extensive collection of intricate and expensive jewellery, furs and collectables, consoled her in her hour of need, but deep down what she missed most of all… was the company of a husband.

Now aged seventy-five, Eleanor once again sought the assistance of the Twilight Romantics Dating Agency in finding husband number three. Why not, she mused? After all… Elizabeth Taylor had had *seven* husbands in her lifetime – why shouldn't *she*?

It wasn't long before Eleanor thought that she had found the perfect prospect.

Gerald Simpson was a retired bank manager looking for that special someone to spend the rest of his life with. A widower for the past twelve years, he was lonely and missed the allure and comfort of female companionship. Alright, he was a little unsteady on his feet, and needed a walking cane for support, but, more importantly, he had a house, and a decent nest egg that he had accumulated over the years. For Eleanor, Gerald seemed to tick all the boxes.

It was a match made in heaven.

It was after several dates that Gerald finally plucked up the courage and popped the question that Eleanor had long been waiting for. They were on The London Eye, when Gerald sat next to Eleanor and proposed, offering a relatively small diamond engagement ring, compared to Dudley's, but such considerations were of minor significance in the grand scheme of things after all. Eleanor overcame her initial disappointment, regained her composure, and said: 'Yes.' The others in the capsule clapped and offered their congratulations. It was an auspicious start to what would turn out to be anything but.

It was six months after the newlyweds had tied the knot, and, through Eleanor's persistence, wills and life-insurance policies safely secured, that the wheels began to fall off their proverbial marriage wagon. It started with Gerald's incessant snoring. Eleanor was unable to sleep because of the noise emanating from Gerald's facial orifice, and if she didn't get at least eight hours of uninterrupted beauty sleep, she was like a bear with a sore head. To Gerald's dismay, Eleanor had become an eight-foot grizzly. The die was cast.

Eleanor relegated her husband to another bedroom to ensure her uninterrupted eight hours of slumber. Gerald noticed that his wife now took to wearing a white face mask while she slept, giving her the impression of a corpse that had long overstayed its welcome. This was not what he had signed up for. On the rare occasion when he would enter her bedroom with amorous intentions, he was stopped in his tracks by the sight of that ghostly apparition lying there before him. He invariably thought better of it and would return to his lonely room, dejected, frustrated, and forlorn.

It was on a Sunday morning, whilst Eleanor was happily listening to the omnibus edition of The Archers on the radio, that Gerald summoned up sufficient fortitude to ask Eleanor for a divorce.

To Eleanor, the very notion of the D word had never made an entrance into her limited vocabulary. It was a word that meant failure, indignity, and… more importantly, a lack of economic return on her investment. No, she insisted, it was out of the question. Why, she wouldn't be able to show her face at the bridge club if she was a divorcee. How selfish of him to even *consider* such a proposition. Didn't he realise the *strain* a divorce would cause to her fragile constitution? The very idea. No. No. No.

The writing was on the wall.

Five weeks later…

'Good morning, Charlie. Good morning, Dudley. Good morning, Gerald.' Eleanor, feather duster in hand, was carefully dusting the three urns that sat majestically upon the mantlepiece above the fireplace. She thought back to the service held at the crematorium for her dearly-departed Gerald, and smiled whimsically at how moving the ceremony was. The service, as usual, only had a few attendees, but the atmosphere rendered by the music and solemnity of the occasion was such that she even had to dramatically dab away a tear that had escaped from her eye and ran delicately down her cheek. Others found this most moving, and proof of the enormity of her sad loss.

She recalled the coroner's verdict of accidental death. The injuries that Gerald sustained, he said, were in accordance with a frail old man who had lost his footing whilst walking down the stairs. He offered Eleanor his heartfelt sympathies for the loss of her loved one, and Eleanor in return was yet again *very* appreciative, if not a little relieved.

It was several months later, just as Eleanor was dipping into a tub of beluga caviar, that she felt the old familiar pang of loneliness once more intrude upon her soul, like a moth to a flame. She needed to be married and there was no time like the present. She felt that she had passed the respectable period of grieving expected for a woman in her prime of life, and, after all, this wasn't the Victorian age, when a much longer period of mourning would have been more socially acceptable. Reviewing the Twilight Romantics Dating Agency's website, Eleanor thought that she had hit the jackpot. His name was Reginald Haverstock-Jennings, and he was a retired Major General in his mid-seventies. He had a lot of letters after his name, which impressed her no end. He was also a widower, three times over, and like Eleanor lived in Eastbourne, so they already had a lot in common with each other. He was independently well off due to shrewd investments that he had made in the stock market.

Eleanor almost had to pinch herself to prove that she wasn't dreaming. It seemed to be the perfect match.

Their first date was a sumptuous dinner at a top Italian restaurant by the coast. Eleanor found Reginald to be charming. He looked every inch a Major General, and had a fine military-bearing moustache beneath a nose that would have been a proud feature for any self-respecting Roman emperor. His deep blue eyes were attentive, and his hair, although grey, was suitably well groomed, and luxuriant. The precise way he ate his linguine with his fork, without spillage, was enacted with military precision, and it sealed the deal for her as a prospective husband number four.

Reginald was old school; whenever he and Eleanor went out on a date, he would escort her to her door, and offer her his arm in support, like the gentleman that he was. He was well turned out in a smart suit, white shirt with a tie that bore his regiment's insignia, and black shoes that were immaculately polished as is customary for an old warrior. He would regale Eleanor with his tales of derring-do while he was in command of his regiment in places such as Iraq, Afghanistan and Northern Ireland. He showed her his collection of medals for bravery and service, as well as a scar that he had received from hand-to-hand combat with the enemy.

It was just a few months later that Reginald popped the question that Eleanor had waited for.

Eleanor enjoyed the title of Mrs Eleanor Haverstock-Jennings. There was a certain element of class in having a double-barrelled surname, and Eleanor would metaphorically bathe in the radiance that the elevated status seemed to evoke in her. Oh, it may seem pretentious, she thought, but first impressions last as they say, and she found that others were often impressed by such seemingly shallow considerations.

Reginald gladly agreed to the drawing up of wills and life insurance – he even suggested a higher payout than Eleanor had recommended, in the event of his, or her, unexpected departure, even if it meant a higher premium; they both agreed that they were no longer spring chickens, and it made perfect sense to compensate for any unforeseen circumstance. He found it odd that Eleanor kept the ashes of her three husbands on the mantlepiece, like trophies, but decided that her eccentricity, although unusual, was even a little endearing.

Unlike her first three husbands, Reginald could dance. He would glide her effortlessly around the dance floor, and, when they were foxtrotting the night away, she felt as though she was Ginger Rogers to his Fred Astaire. His dexterity, for an elderly gentleman, was a treat to behold, and it made her feel young again. He even joined her bridge club, and was a first-rate player, always popular with the other members of the club, especially the *female* members, who were enchanted by his panache and military bearing; Reginald would tease them mercilessly, and Eleanor would laugh it off as innocent flirtation by a man who was a committed husband and a gentleman – after all, she concluded, he was a retired Major General, and they would *never* dream of bringing dishonour to their rank.

All seemed to be going swimmingly between them, until Eleanor noticed that Reginald was going out for long walks on his own more and more lately. He said he enjoyed the exercise, and liked to keep the old joints from seizing up. Eleanor thought nothing of it at first, as he was usually back within the hour, but now he was gone for two to three hours at a time, and she began to get more than a little curious after a while, and knowing Reginald's propensity to flirt, her suspicions intensified like a volcano on the verge of eruption.

Eleanor was not used to the idea that she was no longer the centre of her universe, and it cut deep.

It was the very next morning, after she had finished dusting off her three late husbands, and listened to The Archers on the radio, that she decided to take affirmative action. Reginald was in the back garden, busily mowing the lawn, and had left his mobile phone on the kitchen table. Eleanor took the opportunity that presented itself, and looked at

Reginald's texts. What she found shocked her to the core. Not only was Reginald having an extra-marital dalliance with *one* lady friend, but she discovered that there were *others*. To Eleanor's eternal displeasure, Reginald was a veritable geriatric Casanova.

As Reginald re-entered the kitchen, having worked up quite a sweat, Eleanor quickly, and nonchalantly, put the phone back down on the table, and smiled sweetly at her husband, as though nothing was out of the ordinary. It was a smile that excluded warmth and sincerity – the sort of smile that a spider might give while slowly approaching a fly that had been caught in its web.

It wasn't going to end well…

It was a day as dark as night. The wind howled like tortured souls seeking redemption, and the trees swayed in unison, threatening imminent collapse. The rain splattered against the windows of the crematorium, as if trying to cleanse the scent of an evil spirit that lurked within, while sporadic flashes of lightning lit the external landscape of countless headstones of the long dead. The service was sparsely attended, and as solemn as the weather.

Upon the mantlepiece, above the fireplace, there were now four urns…

'Good morning, Charlie. Good morning, Dudley. Good morning, Gerald,' and as an afterthought: 'Good morning, Eleanor.'

Reginald smiled a sickly-sweet smile that contained no generosity of spirit. He knew from experience that he had been compelled to expedite her departure when he did, before she expedited *his*. After all, it took a serial killer to recognise a fellow serial killer. She was good, he thought to himself, but when he happened to see her looking at his mobile phone, he could tell that his goose was cooked.

The house now belonged solely to him, as planned, which left only the cheque from the proceeds of the life insurance to arrive; it had been a few months now, but he was confident that his bank balance would be sufficiently swollen before long – besides, the coroner conceded that Eleanor had died from natural causes brought on by foolishly ingesting mushrooms that she had gathered from the local woods – a variety that turned out to be deadly poisonous. Who would have thought?

Reginald's real name was Jimmy Alfred Crompton. Reginald Haverstock-Jennings was an assumed identity that he had stolen years ago. Learning how to be a Major General was a huge undertaking, but as a former actor he took to it like a duck to water, adopting the correct mannerisms and storylines that seemed authentic enough to be believable.

Jimmy was a serial philanderer who plundered the wealth of his three previous victims through marriage. Eleanor was a particularly wealthy widow that he had found in the Twilight Romantics Dating Agency, and he had felt that he had hit the jackpot with her, and could at last comfortably retire and enjoy the fruits of his labour in some style with a wide variety of female admirers.

The doorbell rang. Hopefully, he thought, it would be the postman with a fat cheque for him.

As he opened the door, he saw two men formally attired in suits standing before him. The taller man spoke: 'Are you mister Haverstock-Jennings?'

'Yes?'

As the two men flashed their police identity badges, Jimmy felt a sick feeling begin to gnaw in his stomach.

'I wonder if we might have a word?'

A Flicker of Light in the Shadows

The Mulhamptons seemed to have it all. Richard and Wendy, a married couple in their early thirties, lived in a detached Victorian cottage in the rural village of Rimmingdale, North Yorkshire. They were lucky, as the previous owners of the cottage, a young family who had to move because of work commitments, were happy with a quick sale. It was a remote location with more sheep than people, but the calmness and serenity of the area was a welcome relief from the hustle and bustle of their former life in London, two years ago. The contrast was significant. A small church was the closest building to them, and their nearest neighbours were a mile away.

As a successful novelist, Richard found that the tranquillity of the area was a shot in the arm to his creativity, and the words would somehow flow seamlessly onto the blank screen of his laptop with apparent ease. Wendy worked as Richard's editor, ironing out grammatical errors, and occasionally re-writing passages of work that she felt necessary, with his approval. By all appearances they seemed to have the ideal life – after all, they owned their cottage outright, had some money in the bank, and the future seemed promising. But there was one thing that so far had eluded them: a child. They both had siblings, and they knew the importance and stability that family life can bring, so when Wendy announced one morning that she was pregnant, they were both overjoyed.

Life seemed idyllic. It was proof that you *can* have your cake and eat it, as they say, but little did they know of the trauma that lay ahead for them.

Wendy had a good pregnancy; she was a very proud expectant mother, and Richard supported her diligently and devotedly. When their daughter arrived in the county hospital, later that year, they named the child Elizabeth, after Wendy's late mother. Although neither Richard or Wendy held any strong religious affiliation, they decided to arrange a christening at the local parish church of St Mary. Richard's parents and brother attended, as did Wendy's father and sister. A few people from the local community were also there. The parish priest, Reverend Darcey, a tall balding man in his seventies, performed the christening, and duly anointed Elizabeth Mulhampton with holy water which sealed the deal. Both parents were as proud as punch, and felt that they had made a formal connection with the local community.

Five years went by, and all seemed well. Richard had added three novels to his repertoire that were successfully published, and Wendy maintained her work as Richard's editor, in addition to being a full-time mother to their daughter Elizabeth. They had the usual stress that all parents have but, all in all, they felt that they were blessed with good fortune. Elizabeth was the perfect daughter; she had her mother's long auburn hair, intense lilac eyes, and was exceptionally bright for her age. It was shortly after her fifth birthday that the unexpected events began.

It was around two o'clock in the morning that they first heard Elizabeth talking. Woken from her slumber, Wendy went softly into Elizabeth's room, and found her standing beside her bed, staring blankly ahead into the darkness. Her gaze was fixated on something or some*one*. Wendy assumed that her daughter was having a bad dream, and had got up from her bed, transfixed through fright, looking directly ahead of her. Wendy gently put her arm around Elizabeth's shoulder, and carefully led her back to her bed.

She sat for a while beside her, stroking her hair, until Elizabeth fell fitfully asleep. Wendy thought little of the incident that night, and dismissed it as merely a bad dream.

Little did she know that it was the start of things to come.

The next morning, while all three were sat at the kitchen table, eating breakfast, Wendy brought up the previous night's events with her daughter.

'Do you remember why you were standing by your bed, last night?'

'She wanted me to come out and play,' replied Elizabeth, casually.

'*Who* did?' asked Richard, nearly choking on his toast.

'A girl… She said her name was Alison.'

Richard and Wendy looked at each other with concern etched in their eyes. It was Wendy who spoke first.

'It was just a dream,' she said, trying hard to sound comforting. 'We all have dreams that sometimes seem very real.'

'It *was* real, mummy.'

There was something very sincere in Elizabeth's eyes that told her mother that whatever she saw was real to her. Wendy smiled a motherly smile, and stroked her daughter's hair.

'If you've finished your breakfast,' said Richard, 'then get ready for school.' He looked at the clock on the wall. 'It starts in half an hour. You don't want to be late.'

As Wendy drove her daughter to school that morning, the previous night's event weighed heavily upon her mind. Was Elizabeth sleepwalking? She had read somewhere that certain people are able to sleep with their eyes open, and even subconsciously get up and walk about without waking themselves up. She dismissed the idea as unlikely because Elizabeth had always been a sound sleeper. Besides, she reasoned, everybody has experienced dreams that seem so real. It will probably just be a one-off. Nothing to worry about, I'm sure, she thought.

Two days passed and all seemed well, but later that evening, while his wife and daughter were still sleeping, Richard was still in his study, working on his latest novel, late into the night. Unusually, for him, he struggled to find the words necessary to fill the blank screen before him. He removed his glasses, and rubbed his tired eyes. Think I must be getting old, he thought, as he leant wearily back in his seat and massaged his scalp beneath his thick black hair, with the fingers of both hands. He had learned from experience that you can't force the words to come – sometimes it's best just to take a break and try another time. He switched off his laptop, got up, and turned off the light to his study. It was a clear night outside, and the moon cast its faint glow through the black curtains. It was then that he heard the church bell in the distance strike two o'clock. That's odd, he thought, he'd never heard the bell ring in the early hours of the morning before. As he approached the bathroom, to take a shower, he thought he heard his daughter's voice coming from her room. He walked to Elizabeth's room, and gently opened her door. He saw her in the darkness, standing beside her bed, looking directly ahead of her.

'I can't play with you. Not today,' she said, in a voice that was calm.

Richard wanted to switch on the light, and comfort his little girl, but he knew that it was dangerous to wake someone if they were sleepwalking, so he approached his daughter slowly, and gently led her back to her bed. He stayed with her until she was safely fast asleep.

For the rest of the night, as he lay in bed next to his wife, Richard's mind was troubled. He heard the church bell strike three o'clock. As he fell in and out of sleep, visions of the old church nearby, illuminated by the moonlight, entered his weary mind. He saw himself standing in the church graveyard. Vague figures, young and old, dressed in pale clothes from another age, rose from their resting places, and walked towards him. Unable to move, Richard was now surrounded by the walking dead; he felt himself falling slowly down and down into the abyss, and as he looked up, he could see that the ghostly figures were each throwing soil over his helpless figure, until he could see no more.

Richard woke with a start, drenched in sweat. He determined that the bell ringing from the church had something to do with his daughter's strange behaviour. They shouldn't be ringing the bell in the early hours of the morning, he concluded, and he was going to give them a piece of his mind.

Later that morning, while Wendy was taking Elizabeth to school, Richard took the opportunity to walk to the parish church of St Mary, which was less than a mile away. Although he had lived in Rimmingdale for over five years, he had never visited the church before, except for Elizabeth's christening. Perhaps being a lapsed christian, and doubting one's faith, prevented him from crossing the threshold of a church – a sort of religious guilt trip perhaps?

As he approached the church, the graveyard was as Richard envisioned it in his strange dream, minus the ghostly figures that inhabited it. Like most mid-Victorian churches, St Mary had a high pointed steeple, even for a relatively small village church, and gothic-styled stained-glass windows. Perched on the edges of the roof were several hideous gargoyles depicting devilish creatures of various guises, which gave the church a surreal haunting look from a bygone age.

As Richard entered the church, there was no one to be seen. The interior of the church was deceptively spacious, and as he walked down the aisle towards the pulpit, he could hear his own footsteps echo against the flint walls. Apart from oil paintings of Mary Magdelene and Jesus on a cross, there were few artifacts within the church. As he reached the pulpit, to his right was the baptismal font which brought back happy memories of Elizabeth's christening.

Suddenly, a door to the left opened, and Reverend Darcey made an entrance. He was informally dressed in white shirt with an ecclesiastical collar, black trousers, and a comfortable pair of old shoes. When he spoke, he sounded slightly out of breath.

'I *thought* I heard somebody,' he said. 'Have you been waiting long?'

'No reverend. I've just got here.'

'I was just tending to sandwiches, in preparation for the local book club later. We make up for the reduced congregation by getting more involved with community projects these days.' He had a wistful look in his eyes. 'That's progress, I suppose… We used to pack 'em in back in the old days. But that was then… Are you here for private devotion, Mister…?'

'Mulhampton. Richard Mulhampton. And no.'

'Mulhampton… Ah, yes. I performed a baptism. For your daughter. Elizabeth, as I recall?'

'That's right.'

'I'm afraid my memory isn't quite as sharp as it used to be. I used to remember *all* my congregation years ago. All their names. Even where they lived. Sadly, so many people leave the parish these days. They come and go. Especially young people. Off to the bright lights of the city, I suppose?'

'I've come about the church bell.'

'Are you a campanologist?'

'Hmm?'

'Bell ringer.'

'Oh... no. It's about the bell being rung in the early hours of the morning. I think it's been having a detrimental effect on our daughter's sleep pattern.'

'You must be mistaken,' said the priest. 'You see, the laws are pretty strict when it comes to church bells. Our last session is at eight o'clock in the evening. Of course, there are exceptions such as wedding ceremonies, but at no time would we ring the bells in the early hours of the morning.'

Richard looked at the priest incredulously. 'But that's not possible,' he said. 'I heard them with my own ears. As clear as a...'

'Bell?'

'Yes.'

'Sometimes,' said the priest, 'the mind can play tricks on us. Things that seem so real can be the result of... stress. Often times alcohol.'

'I don't drink. I *know* what I heard,' said Richard, mildly irritated.

'Tell me, Mister Mulhampton, what work do you do?'

'I'm a writer.'

'I see... I would imagine that must be a very stressful occupation at times?'

Richard nodded. 'It can be. At times... Especially when you have writer's block.'

'And did you last night? Have writer's block?'

'I did, but-'

'Then you must concede that it's a possibility, Mister Mulhampton?'

Even Richard was starting to doubt his own ears. 'I suppose it's a possibility,' he said. 'But it seemed so real.'

'Perhaps you're worrying unnecessarily?'

'But my daughter... She's started sleepwalking. We've found her standing by her bed talking to an imaginary girl called Alison.'

The revelation piqued the priest's interest. 'Oh? Alison, you say?'

Richard was surprised by his reaction. 'Does that mean something to you?' he asked.

The priest shook his head, slowly but not convincingly. 'I'm sure it's nothing. You live at Pemberwick Cottage, is that right?'

'That's right. How did you know?'

'I've made it my practice, over the years, to know who my neighbours are, Mister Mulhampton, even if they don't attend my sermons. My clergy house is a bit further up the road from here.

Richard felt the flush of guilt that many who have lost faith feel. 'It's not you, reverend,' he started to say.

'I'm pulling your leg. It's for a power far higher than mine to invigorate your faith. It's always a personal choice. Not one that should be mandatory by any means... Although it would have been nice to have got a full congregation now and then, before I retire.'

'You're leaving the parish?'

'This will be my last year. I've served this community for over forty years.'

'Any regrets?'

Richard noticed a look of resignation in the priest's eyes.

'We all have regrets, Mister Mulhampton,' he said, wearily. 'Now, if you'll excuse me, I must get back to my preparations for the book club.'

'Yes. Of course. Sorry to have taken so much of your time.'

Richard started to walk out of the church.

'Oh, Mister Mulhampton?'

He stopped and turned to the priest. 'Yes, reverend?'

'How old is your daughter now?'

'She turned five about a week ago.'

Richard carried on walking, and left the church.

Reverend Darcey looked on. A look of concern was now growing in his eyes. 'Oh dear,' he said to himself. 'It's happening again…'

A month passed without incident, and all seemed well. It was a Saturday afternoon, and Wendy was in the kitchen, preparing lunch, while Elizabeth sat at the dining table, busily drawing pictures in her sketchbook, with her coloured pencils.

'Lizzy,' called Wendy. 'Can you go upstairs, and tell daddy that lunch is ready, please?'

'But I want to finish my drawing.'

'*Now* please.'

Elizabeth reluctantly put down her coloured pencil. 'Okay,' she huffed.

She rose from the table, and ran upstairs to Richard's study. Wendy had made a ploughman's lunch for each of them, and now entered the dining room, and put the plates of food on the table. Her daughter was still upstairs with Richard, when Elizabeth's sketch pad caught her eye; she picked it up and looked at what her daughter had been drawing. The pad was full of roughly drawn pictures of a girl in a nightdress, in various shades of colour. At first, Wendy thought nothing of it as they were the usual crudely drawn outlines from a young child's mind, but underneath several of the pictures was the name, barely legible: Alison.

Wendy's heart sank. She tried to dismiss it from her mind – after all, she thought, small children often have imaginary friends. Perhaps she was worrying unnecessarily?

Richard came into the dining room, holding Elizabeth in his arm. He could see that his wife was distraught but trying hard not to show it; she had Elizabeth's sketch pad in her hand, and she was looking to him with a worried look in her eyes. Richard put Elizabeth down. 'Let's eat,' he said.

Wendy put the sketch pad back down on the table, and they each sat down and began to eat.

'Have you seen Lizzy's pictures?' Wendy asked Richard.

'No? Are they good?'

'Why don't you show daddy your pictures, Lizzy?'

Elizabeth happily picked up her sketch pad, and proudly passed it to her father.

Richard flicked through the pages of the pad. He was mesmerised by what he saw. He glanced at Wendy. A worried look gathered in his eyes, but he tried to supress his concerns for the benefit of his daughter's feelings. 'These are very good pictures, Lizzy,' he said. 'You've coloured them in beautifully. You haven't gone over the lines at all. Who are they of?'

'My friend, Alison,' she replied, matter-of-factly, and carried on eating her lunch.

Richard and Wendy exchanged anxious looks.

'Alison?' said Richard, sheepishly. 'Is that somebody at your school?'

'Oh no. We play in my room.'

'And what do you play up there, Lizzy?' asked Wendy. There was a slight tremble in her voice.

'Dolls,' said Elizabeth. 'Alison likes teddy. She said she never had one so I let her play with him.' She looked at her parents and could tell that they were not happy. 'Did I do wrong?'

Wendy could see that Elizabeth was about to cry, so she tried to comfort her. 'No, sweetheart. You didn't do anything wrong. Eat your lunch.'

Wendy and Richard exchanged a brief look that spoke of their dread, and then they carried on eating as though nothing had happened.

Later that afternoon, while Wendy and Elizabeth were at the shops, Richard was in the kitchen preparing coffee, when the doorbell rang. He wasn't expecting any visitors, and he very nearly didn't answer it. As a writer he worked more productively when in quiet solitude, but his curiosity got the better of him, and so he reluctantly opened the front door. Standing before him, in his clerical attire, was the priest.

'Reverend Darcey. I wasn't expecting you.'

'Hello Mister Mulhampton. May I come in?'

'Yes, of course.' Richard stood aside and let the priest in. 'I was just making coffee. Would you like a cup?'

'That would be splendid. Black and sweet please, if it's not too much trouble?'

Richard led the priest into the dining room, and invited him to sit at the table, while he returned to the kitchen to make coffee. 'What brings you here, reverend?' Richard called from the kitchen.

'Tomorrow will be my last day at St Mary,' he said.

Richard brought in their cups of coffee, and put them down upon the table. He sat opposite the priest. 'Tomorrow?'

'Yes. Reverend Seabody will take over the reins. He's a fine young priest. I'm sure he will be a credit to the community of Rimmingdale.'

'I'm sure the people of the village are going to miss you,' said Richard, warmly. 'I hope you enjoy your retirement.'

'Thank you... You know, Mister Mulhampton, it would mean the world to me if you and your family would attend my final sermon tomorrow morning?'

Richard thought it through. 'I'm sure we can arrange that,' he said.

'Splendid.' It was then that the priest noticed Elizabeth's sketch pad lying on the table; it was open and revealing her latest drawings. 'Is this your daughter's?'

'I think she's allowed her imagination to get the better of her,' said Richard, sipping his coffee.

The priest picked up the sketch pad. 'May I?' he asked.

'Of course.'

'These are very good,' said the priest. 'Especially for her age.' As he slowly leafed through the pad, his expression became more and more serious.

Richard could tell that the priest was perturbed. 'Is there something wrong, reverend?'

The priest looked up at Richard. 'Mister Mulhampton,' he said, solemnly, 'I haven't been entirely truthful with you, to my eternal shame.'

'I don't understand?'

The priest looked pensive. 'That day that you came into the church…'

'Yes?'

'It was then that I realised…'

There was a palpable silence in the air, broken by Richard. 'Realised what?' he prompted.

The priest looked to Richard with an earnest expression growing in his eyes. 'When you bought Pemberwick Cottage, it was a quick sale?'

'Yes. We were very lucky. They needed to sell quickly, so we took advantage of it.'

The priest took a moment of careful deliberation before he responded. 'Did you ever wonder why they were so keen for a quick sale?'

'I don't think we gave it much thought. We were too pleased to seal the deal.'

'Yes. Of course… Tell me, Mister Mulhampton, do you believe in restless spirits?'

The priest's question took Richard by surprise. 'I'm not sure I know what you mean,' he said.

'A poor soul who is locked in a moment of transition before finding the eternal light.'

'Like a ghost, you mean?'

The priest nodded solemnly. ''It's a personal belief. It's not scripture, and it's not in religious teaching, that's for sure, but there are, I believe, for whatever reasons, examples that manifest themselves in unusual ways. I believe that your daughter has experienced just such a manifestation.'

'How can you be sure?'

The priest gave Richard's reservation careful deliberation. 'Because I know who Alison is… or rather… *was*.'

Richard was almost lost for words. This was too much for him to take in. 'Who *was* she?' he managed to blurt out.

'Her name was Alison Pemberwick, and her remains were buried in St Mary's cemetery.'

'Pemberwick?'

The priest nodded. 'My predecessor, Reverend Johnson, told me about her when I first became the clergyman of the church, many years ago. It's a tale that has been handed down over the years since the late-Victorian age. Her family bought your cottage when it was first built. She was five years old when a fire broke out in her bedroom, believed to be caused by a lit candle that was left unattended. The poor soul died.

Richard could feel the hairs on the back of his neck stand up. 'Incredible,' he murmured. 'But why are you telling me this now?'

'I suppose because I couldn't live with myself if I neglected to tell you of the full story of Alison, as it was relayed to me. I thought it best that you know before I leave for pastures new.'

As Richard sat in his study later that evening, he recalled the priest's strange tale. He decided not to tell Wendy, as he believed it would only worry her unnecessarily. He couldn't sleep that night thinking of that poor girl who died a wretched death at such a young age. Occasionally, during that long restless evening, he would look in on his daughter.

Thankfully Elizabeth was sleeping peacefully, and did so throughout the night. Richard decided that it would be fitting that they all attend Reverend Darcey's last sermon the next day, and his wife agreed.

It was a beautiful sunny day. The church had a large congregation of villagers who had come out in order to pay their respects to their priest who had served them so faithfully for such a long time. Richard, Wendy, and Elizabeth, who was clutching her favourite teddy bear closely to her chest, all sat at the front of the congregation to listen to the sermon. The priest's words were rich with the values of goodness, fairness, neighbourly support for one another. And love.

When the sermon was over, Reverend Darcey stood at the church vestibule meeting each member of the congregation as they left, wishing them all luck, and receiving warm gratitude in return for all his efforts over the years, and how he would be missed as a member of their community. Richard, Wendy, and Elizabeth were the last of the congregation to pay their last respects to the priest. Reverend Darcey shook Richard's hand firmly, and then Wendy's. He looked down at their daughter with a fatherly tenderness.

'You must be Elizabeth?' he said, and shook the little girl's hand. 'I haven't seen you since you were a baby. My, how you've grown.'

Elizabeth looked up to the priest. 'I'm five,' she said, proudly.

'Really? My goodness, you're growing up fast.' He looked to Richard. 'Come with me, all of you, there's something I would like you to see.'

The priest took Elizabeth by the hand, and they each followed him, not knowing what to expect.

As they walked slowly through the cemetery, they came to a stop at an old gravestone that had been severely tainted by the effects of mother nature, but the occupant's name was still legible: Alison Pemberwick. As they stood beside the gravestone, the priest took out a small bottle from his vestment pocket, and opened its lid.

'If you would indulge me,' he said calmly to the others. 'I thought we would say a little prayer for the benefit of the deceased, Alison, whose remains lie before us now, and to sanctify her place of rest with holy water.' Richard and Wendy, as well as Reverend Darcey, each closed their eyes. Elizabeth tried to close her eyes, but couldn't resist peeking now and then, as she was excited to be a part of something that grown-ups do; without forethought she placed her teddy bear upon the gravestone, and briefly closed her eyes again. The priest carefully sprayed some of the water over the gravestone, and began his prayer: 'God our Father, in this sacred place – this hallowed ground, and in the presence of your love, we pray for all our loved ones buried here. We ask that you continue to enfold them in your mercy, love and peace, through our Lord Jesus Christ, your Son, who lives and reigns with you, in the unity of the Holy Spirit, one God for ever and ever. Amen.'

As Elizabeth opened her eyes once more, she could clearly see the brief vision of a young girl standing before her. She had long dark hair, and was dressed in a nightgown that went down to her ankles. She was smiling sweetly at Elizabeth, and for reasons unknown, Elizabeth didn't feel scared or intimidated in the slightest – in fact she instinctively felt a calmness and serenity envelop her, and she knew that all was well and would continue to be well for now and forever more. The vision slowly faded, and disappeared for eternity.

A Student of Death

Pamela Henney had found the Ouija board in the bottom of a cupboard, probably left by a former student in her small college residence. As she waited for her four friends, who were fellow students, to turn up for Halloween festivities, she placed the board in the middle of her small round table. She then positioned chairs, that she had mostly borrowed from her neighbours, around the table. She had a couple of bottles of wine in the kitchen as well as a few snacks, and had asked that the others bring a bottle with them. It was to be a boozy affair.

Pamela was one of life's organisers. Every group of friends seemed to have at least one, somebody who is good at arranging gatherings, and is the glue that keeps it all together. Tall and sporty, with short blonde hair, Pamela was often considered by the others to be the tomboy of the group.

They were each in their first year at Summerlee College, West Sussex, studying for business degrees which they hoped would eventually gain them entry into a worthwhile job.

The first to arrive was Carl Evans. Short with thick black hair and stubbled chin, he was known as the joker in the pack with an outgoing personality. He held a bottle of red wine in his hand.

'Attended a lecture on scientific management earlier,' he said. 'The only saving grace was that Professor Wilkinson was dressed up as Dracula. It was quite a sight.' He lifted the bottle up. 'Hope this cheap plonk is okay? It's about all I could afford. Bit skint at the moment. Tim still hasn't paid me that tenner he owes.'

'I'm sure it's fine,' said Pamela. 'We're not known for having a discerning palate.'

Carl spots the Ouija board on the table. 'Oh sweet. Where did you get that from? Looks pretty old.'

Pamela took the bottle from Carl, and made her way to the kitchen. 'Found it in the cupboard when I first got here,' she said. 'Thought we could have some fun with it. Grab a seat. The others should be here soon.'

Carl sat at the table, and looked at the large dark oblong wooden board before him; it had the capital letters of the alphabet in lines from left to right, and numbers from one to twenty underneath. On the top left corner of the board was the word YES, and in the top right corner NO. Bottom left corner was HELLO, and bottom right GOODBYE. A separate heart-shaped piece of wood, on casters, was in the middle of the board – it had a large hole at its point.

Pamela came back into the room, bearing two full glasses of wine. She sat down opposite Carl, and passed him a glass.

'Thanks,' he said, and took a large gulp of wine. 'I've never used a Ouija board before… You?'

Pamela shook her head. 'Can't be too difficult. As I understand it, you ask if a spirit's here, and then ask it lots of questions. We each put a finger on the planchette-'

'Planchette? What's that when it's at home?'

'This heart-shaped piece of wood,' she replied.

There was a knock at the door. Pamela got up and opened it. Belinda James and Tim Delaine let themselves in. Each was carrying a bottle of wine. Pamela took the bottles, and went into the kitchen. 'Make yourselves at home,' she said.

Belinda and Tim joined Carl at the table. They were both quite tall. Belinda styled herself as a goth – she wore a black loose-fitting dress, had long black hair, matching eye make-up, and a silver ring through her lip. Tim had long scraggly blonde hair, and was casually dressed in dark t-shirt and ripped jeans.

'Oh sweet,' gushed Belinda. 'You've got a Ouija board. That's right up my street.'

'Let's hope we don't mistake you for a ghost,' ventured Carl.

'Cheeky bastard,' replied Belinda, half-jokingly.

Carl turned his attention to Tim. He didn't need to say anything.

'I'll have it for you by end of week. Things are a bit tight at the moment.'

Carl smiled. 'Tell me about it,' he said.

Pamela came back into the room holding two glasses of wine, which she gave to Belinda and Tim.

The last to arrive was Samantha Dodgeson. With clipped red hair, and wearing a smart black suit, with white blouse, Samantha looked more like an executive director of a law firm rather than a college student. She held a shopping bag in her hand.

'Ah,' said Carl. 'The late Samantha Dodgeson.'

'Don't mind him,' said Pamela. 'Let me get you some wine.'

'Thanks,' said Samantha. She passed Pamela her bag. 'I've brought a couple of bottles of red for good measure.'

'Great. The more the merrier. I'll take them off your hands. Grab a seat.'

Pamela went to the kitchen.

Samantha joined the others at the table. 'What's all this then?' she said, looking at the Ouija board, with interest.

'It's a delve into the dark arts,' said Belinda. 'Do you believe in the afterlife?' she asked.

Samantha considered at length. 'Not sure that it's been scientifically proven. But I'm willing to keep an open mind.'

Pamela re-emerged from the kitchen, with a glass of wine, and handed it to Samantha. She lit the candles with a lighter, switched off the main light, and then sat down with the others. 'If anybody needs topping up,' she said, 'the booze is in the kitchen – help yourselves. I've made some snacks for later.'

'How do we start?' asked Tim.

'We each put a finger on the planchette,' replied Pamela. 'And then we ask the spirit world questions.'

'Can we ask it when Tim is going to pay me back that tenner he owes?'

Tim gave Carl a stern look of rebuke.

They all placed a finger on the planchette. The only pale light in the room now came from the candles, which leant the proceedings an eerie atmosphere.

'Who wants to ask the questions?' asked Pamela.

Belinda was the first to chip in. 'I'll ask,' she said, eagerly, and paused momentarily before saying, loudly: 'Spirit world – is there anyone here with us now?'

The planchette remained motionless at first, but then, after a moment's hesitation, moved sporadically around the Ouija board, in a violent manner, as if possessed.

'Christ!' exclaimed Tim.

Samantha admonished him. 'Ssh Tim! Let's hear what the spirit has to say.'

The planchette eventually went to the top left of the Ouija board: YES.

'What is your name, spirit?' asked Belinda, with a slight tremor in her voice.

The planchette moved haphazardly at first but then a name was slowly spelt: D A V I D.

'David,' said Pamela, excitedly. 'His name is David!'

Belinda continued with her questions. 'How old were you, David, when you passed into the spirit world?'

The planchette moved towards the numbers on the board: 2 3.

'Two three. He's twenty-three,' said Pamela.

'*Was*,' corrected Samantha.

'Can you tell us what your last name was, David?' asked Belinda.

The planchette seemed to move more purposefully around the letters of the board and spelt: H A N S O N.

'Hanson. His name was David Hanson,' said Pamela, satisfied that they had got this far.

'And how did you die, David?' asked Belinda.

There was a long hesitation before the planchette started moving swiftly around the board.

'Tim's pushing it!' declared Carl.

'No I'm not!'

'Let's see what the spirit has to say,' said Samantha, mildly annoyed.

The planchette spelt: P O I S O N E D.

'He was poisoned,' said Pamela, looking to the others with dread in her eyes. 'Oh my god.'

'Who poisoned you, David?' asked Belinda, trying to remain calm.

A cold air permeated the room, and the candles started to flicker, as though a window had just been opened.

'What's happening?' said Tim, a note of fear in his voice.

Pamela looked around the room, wide-eyed, as though looking for answers. 'I don't know.'

The planchette started to move, erratically at first, and then with conviction. It spelt: F I N C H L E Y.

'He was poisoned by somebody called Finchley,' said Pamela.

'Poor bastard,' said Carl. 'At twenty-three…'

'Maybe we should stop?' cautioned Tim.

'We can't stop *now*,' enthused Belinda. 'It's just getting interesting!'

'What's the matter, Tim? Scared?' said Carl, bitterly.

'No... Course not...'

Belinda carried on regardless. 'David... What year were you poisoned?'

The planchette hesitated before moving to the numbers: 1 8 9 6.

The others looked at each other frantically. This had suddenly become all too real. An unearthly musty odour entered the room, as though the remains of the deceased were with them now.

'God. That smell!' said Tim, suddenly covering his nose with a tissue.

Shallow breathing echoed throughout the room, barely audible but omnipresent.

'Can anyone else hear that?' asked Carl. The others nodded.

'Eighteen ninety-six,' whispered Pamela, solemnly.

'David,' said Belinda, 'were you a student at this college?'

The planchette moved to the top left of the Ouija board: YES.

'And where were you buried?' she continued.

The planchette moved slowly and deliberately amongst the letters. It spelt: S H A L L O W G R A V E.

Pamela looked up to the others. 'Shallow grave...'

'But *where* David? *Where* is your shallow grave?' asked Belinda.

The planchette spelt: B Y O A K T R E E I N G R O U N D S.

'He's buried by an oak tree in the grounds of the college,' said Pamela.

'Poor soul,' whispered Tim.

'I know where he is,' declared Samantha, enthusiastically, 'there's only one oak tree, and it must be hundreds of years old.'

Belinda asked more questions for David Hanson to answer, but the planchette no longer responded. It was as if they had lost contact with the deceased. The line to the dead was, figuratively speaking, *dead*. All five withdrew their fingers from the planchette. The chill in the air, the shallow breathing, and the strange musty odour, dissipated until a semblance of normality slowly returned to the room.

'Where do we go from here?' asked Carl.

'I think we only have one option,' said Belinda.

Samantha interjected. 'If you're saying what I think you're saying, I'm not sure we can just dig up around the oak tree without permission.'

'What if we do it in the dark?' suggested Tim.

'That might work,' replied Pamela.

Carl had an idea. 'We could borrow a couple of spades from the college gardener. I know where he keeps them.'

'Then it's decided,' said Belinda. 'We'll make an evening of it. And… who knows… maybe we'll get lucky and find what's left of poor David Hanson?'

'We'll be famous!' gushed Tim.

'Or infamous,' countered Carl, trying to remain stoic.

'Are we sure this is what we want to do?' asked Samantha, generally.

'How do you mean?' said Pamela.

'How can we be sure that one of us didn't move the planchette?'

They all looked to each other in silence. Samantha was right. It could have been any one of them. But who? Why? The unravelling of David Hanson's death was so fantastic a tale that it just might have been concocted by any of the five friends. After all, it was Halloween, and people have been known to fabricate tales of the supernatural to impress others. Why would this be any different?

'I'm willing to swear on a stack of bibles that it wasn't me,' said Carl, vehemently.

'Me too,' said Tim.

Pamela was the next to speak. 'I'm willing to swear on my mother's life that it wasn't me.'

'My mother's dead,' said Belinda, 'but I'm willing to swear on my father's life that it wasn't me.'

That only left Samantha. All eyes were on her.

'I'm not religious,' said Samantha, 'so I won't swear on a bible. But I am willing to swear on my family's lives that I did not move that planchette.'

There was a moment of dignified silence amongst the five friends that signified the seriousness of what they had got themselves into. There was no turning back. They were committed...

It was a still, misty night, and the pale glow from the moon lent an air of expectation. The five friends now gathered around the old oak tree that had stood in the college grounds for centuries. They each felt the momentous majesty of the tree, which neither of them had felt before – after all, the tree had withstood the ravages of nature, wars and pestilence, and had survived all that had challenged its very survival. Its strength was palpable. It had outlived generations of people and historical events. Students from a different age, long-since dead, would have sat around its noble trunk, and discussed their hopes and dreams for the future. Lovers, perhaps, from a bygone era, would have exchanged stolen kisses beneath the comfort and shelter of the tree's foliage. If the tree could talk, what secrets could it tell? What wisdom could it impart? Thoughts and unanswered questions entered each of the five as they now stood in quiet contemplation.

Carl and Samantha held spades, while the others held lit candles and bottles of wine, which they occasionally swigged from.

'I feel that we ought to say a few words before we start the dig,' suggested Pamela, who was by now slightly the worse for wear. 'As a way of showing our respect.'

Belinda took it upon herself to speak, in hushed tones. 'Oh, mighty oak tree... forgive our indulgence. With your consent we are here to find the remains of the deceased David Hanson.'

The gentle wind shook the branches of the tree, and the leaves rustled in unison, as though granting permission for the five to dig within its realm.

Carl and Samantha began to dig around the perimeter of the oak tree's trunk. They each took turns to dig, and an hour passed quickly but they found precisely nothing, except for worms and stones of all shapes and sizes.

As Pamela pushed the spade into the earth once more, there was a distinct clunk sound of metal upon metal. 'I seem to have struck something,' she said, excitedly, and continued to dig.

Tim, who held the other spade, began to dig beside Pamela, and soon they could see the outline of a small black metal box, about a foot below the surface. Between them they managed to dislodge the box from its place of burial, and Pamela then picked it up. She looked to the others. A look of bewilderment was written in her eyes. This was not what they were expecting to find – bones perhaps... but not a box? They patted the earth back down as best they could to cover their tracks, and then took the box back to Pamela's college residence, where she laid it on the table upon an old newspaper, beside the Ouija board.

The metal box was smothered in a layer of mud and clay. Pamela set about wiping the box with an old cloth until it was relatively clean. It had the appearance of an old money box that had rusted with age. The lid was firmly locked, so Carl used a screwdriver to try and prise it open. When the lid was finally opened, inside the box they could see that there was a small brown leather pouch. Pamela took out the pouch, and, with some trepidation, opened it; tucked deep inside it was a piece of paper, carefully folded several times. Pamela unfolded the paper, and laid it down upon the table, for all to see. Although stained with age and the elements, the paper had handwriting on it, in ink, which was still legible. They each read, in awe, the contents of the letter which was as follows:

30th October, 1896

Dear Recipient,
If you are reading this, then I am almost certainly no longer of this world.
My name is David Edgar Hanson, and I am a student at Summerlee College, and currently reside in the college's hall of residence. I am twenty-two years of age. I am studying for a degree in law, in accordance with my father's wishes, and this is my last year.
I developed an interest (some might say obsession) in the supernatural world when I discovered a spirit board left by a past tenant in my present abode. When I graduate, I will leave the board for others to indulge themselves in the dark arts, if they are so inclined, as I and four of my fellow students have these past three years.
Please forgive my elaborate ruse. I have taken it upon myself to construct this letter with the intention of concealing it

by the old oak tree in the grounds of the college. My ambition is, when I eventually pass from this physical world to the glorious spiritual, to respond to those engaging the power of the spirit board, with an outlandish tale of my untimely demise by the hand of Finchley. Finchley in London is actually my place of birth, and not my assassin!

I intend to prove the existence of the spiritual world, when I have passed, by returning to the place of my education of which I have fond memories. I have created an intriguing tale of woe that will sufficiently motivate you and others to locate this letter. It means that I have been successful in contacting you from beyond the grave.

I remain your humble correspondent.
D.E. Hanson esq.

When Pamela, Carl, Tim, Belinda and Samantha had each fully read the letter, a dignified silence fell upon the room. Their lives would never be quite the same for this mystical experience.

Upon further research, the five discovered more about David Edgar Hanson – he was a First Lieutenant in the Northumberland Fusiliers during the First World War, and was killed in action in an obscure field in France, during the battle of the Somme in the year nineteen-sixteen...

The Many Lives of Henry

Henry Wilderforce was an unremarkable human being. He had no discernible talent. He wasn't handsome. He wasn't rich. He never married. Retired and elderly, he was one of life's natural loners who was comfortable in his own skin. He went about his day minding his own business, and watched life go on around him like an observer rather than as a participant. People would pass him by without a second glance. But Henry was content being Mister Invisible.

Henry had worked as an accountant for over forty years, and his life now consisted of long walks, shopping, and going to the local library. He was a voracious reader – he had read several novels by Charles Dickens, and now turned his attention to the works of P.G. Wodehouse.

Henry was a thinker. As he now walked the familiar streets of his home town in Kent, he observed the people that walked by, and wondered at the lives they led. They each had a story to tell. The intricacies of life fascinated him. We are all existing in our own time and space, he mused, and when our time is up, we depart this mortal world. Life is strange.

As Henry continued his long walk, the sky noticeably darkened, and the clouds now had an angry look about them. The rain began to fall, slowly at first, and the first crack of thunder could be heard high in the heavens above, but this did not deter Henry. He continued to walk, and allowed the rain to fall upon his thinning grey hair, and over his lined face. Ever since he was a young boy, all those years ago, he had been fascinated by storms, and he enjoyed being out in the worsening weather. The rain came down now a little harder.

Henry looked up at the black sky above just as a flash of lightning enveloped his entire body, in the blink of an eye. It was such a compelling force of nature that Henry didn't even realise that he had been struck. It was as if somebody had suddenly switched off all his senses. He didn't know that an ambulance had picked him up. He didn't know that he was in a hospital bed. He didn't know that he was in a coma…

It could have been hours. It could have been days. It could have been weeks. Henry was existing in a state of limbo. He had lived in darkness for so long, not knowing for sure if he was alive or dead. Perhaps this is what it means to lose one's life? A perpetual state of nothingness? The promised land just an illusion created by mortals with good intentions? He was a prisoner in his own body. Trapped like a fly in a spider's web, unable to escape from whatever fate had in store.

It was during this seemingly interminable state of disrepair that Henry saw a faint light ahead of him. He had read of people on the brink of death who see a strange glow. He speculated that it was probably some chemical reaction in the brain; that it was nature's way of using the few remaining brain cells that still existed. Nevertheless, he was intrigued, and like a moth to a flame he found himself concentrating on the light which grew ever brighter until images, sounds, and even smells, very gradually, became more intense…

It was unmistakeable. Henry could see things through another's eyes. He had no control. He had no say in the matter. And yet there was something that connected him to this other person. But what?

Soon his mind was filled with events that he had only read about in books, and seen in documentaries…

Explosions. The night sky lit up with a violent barrage of missiles overhead. The smell of gunpowder and death filled the air. The young man clung to the mudded wall that offered some protection, and prayed for deliverance. As he looked about him, he could see others also clinging to the embankment. Hundreds of them. They were wearing uniforms, as was he. They all seemed so ridiculously young. Soldiers of the British army, embroiled in a war not of their making. Each soldier held a Lee Enfield rifle, close to their chest, as did he. He saw an officer standing bravely at the top of a makeshift ladder, observing the hell of war before him. He held a pistol in his hand. There was a whistle in his mouth, attached to a chain around his neck. He was waiting for the explosions to abate before giving the command to go over the top. It felt like an eternity.

A fellow soldier to the young man's right spoke to him.

'Looks like this is it, Charlie. Let's give the Hun a taste of their own medicine.'

Charlie looked to his comrade, at first with pity and fear in his eyes, but then he thought of all of his young comrades who had already perished in this god-awful conflict in a foreign land of fields and blood. 'Let's kill as many of those bastards as we can,' he said, with a new-found vengeance, and gripped his rifle more tightly.

The officers screamed the order: 'Fix bayonets!'

Each soldier withdrew bayonets from their belts, and secured them to their rifles. If there was to be close combat, a bayonet can be a formidable weapon at arm's-length.

They awaited the signal to go over the top. What was minutes seemed like hours.

The officers along the tops of the trench blew their whistles long and loud. This was it. The moment of truth. Each soldier calmly climbed out of the trench, and slowly walked towards the enemy's position.

As Charlie walked alongside his comrades, with rifles at the ready, it was a chilling experience. They had to step over corpses that had already succumbed to the devastation, in order to make progress towards the enemy. Machine guns spat their venom among their numbers, and many men fell, dying or dead. They increased their gait and were now much closer to their foe. They began firing their rifles into the darkness, not knowing if their bullets found their target but knowing that the Hun were in that vicinity. Screams of those, friend and foe, filled the air. War was stupid, thought Charlie. What does it ever achieve besides reducing those who were once living, breathing, members of the human race?

An explosion nearby. Charlie was knocked off his feet and now lay helpless. A stretcher-bearer, who Charlie recognised, approached him.

'Private Wilderforce. Are you badly injured?'

Charlie could barely hear him as his eardrums had burst due to the blast. The blood seeping out of his forehead told its own story.

The stretcher-bearer began swiftly wrapping a bandage around Charlie's head. There was no time to delay. He couldn't treat the wound but he had to stop the bleeding, otherwise Charlie would bleed to death.

Darkness...

Henry was an involuntary witness to another's traumatic experience. Was it coincidence that Charlie's surname was the same as his? Was Charlie a blood relative from his line of the family that he never knew existed? There were too many questions left unanswered.

Henry saw a burgeoning light in the distance.

He was in a classroom sitting at a desk. He was very young – perhaps no older than eleven. It was a very old classroom.

A photograph of King Edward VII was on the wall to his left. In front of him was a blackboard on an easel. On the blackboard were the words: *I will not talk in class, as it disrupts other pupils.* A door with the title HEADMASTER emblazoned upon it, was to the right of the blackboard. A female teacher, dressed rather like a suffragette, but without a hat, stood beside him, reviewing what he was writing, in chalk, on his large square slate. She was not impressed.

'That is barely legible. You must keep it neat child, otherwise the headmaster will be especially unimpressed. Do you want to incur the wrath of Mister Jenkins any more than you already have?'

The boy looked up to the teacher. He knew that he was in for a caning before long. 'No miss. Sorry, miss.'

He carried on copying the text on the blackboard, as best he could, but it was an uphill struggle. The thought of receiving corporal punishment from a large bearded man who struck fear in all of the pupils at the school made his hand shake.

The teacher offered her unsolicited advice to the boy. 'Let this be a lesson to you. That it is improper to talk during class, unless you are asked a question. Then it is permissible. Schools have rules that must be upheld, otherwise there is anarchy. Do you know what the meaning of anarchy is?'

'No miss.'

'It is needless disruption. It is a distraction that must be avoided at all times. Do you understand?'

'Yes miss.'

'This is not your first misdemeanour. You do not seem to learn from your past mistakes. Tell me – do you think I take pleasure in seeing you punished?'

'Err… No miss?'

'I assure you that I do not. My time is better spent teaching rather than enforcing retribution.'

The door to the headmaster's office opened. Standing in the doorway was Mister Jenkins, cane in hand at the ready. He looked formidable in his formal black gown. He was so large that there was very little room either side of him.

'Wilderforce,' he simply said, and stepped back into the room to allow the boy to enter.

The boy rose from his seat, with some trepidation, and begrudgingly went into the office. As the boy looked back to the teacher, he could see that there was a noticeable look of concern in her eyes. The headmaster closed the door behind him.

Inside the office the boy leant over the desk. He knew the practice of corporal punishment well enough. The first strike of the cane, as always, took him by surprise in its forcefulness. He tried desperately to block the pain by thinking of happier times, but by the sixth strike tears welled up in his eyes. He determined not to tell his parents of his punishment as they would be disappointed in him.

Darkness…

It was a misty morning. It was very early as there was dew still on the grassy field, and a distinct cool freshness in the air that only comes from the first light of day. The sound of birdsong came from a nearby weeping willow. He was fully dressed in a gentleman's attire for that period of time: white frilled shirt, ornate waistcoat, heavy woollen jacket, wide breeches and laced black leather boots. A younger man stood close at hand. There were three other gentlemen, similarly dressed, and they were all grouped together a short distance away.

The tallest of the three, wearing a top hat, came towards him; he was holding a small case in his hands. 'Are you quite sure that you want to go through with this, Wilderforce?' he asked. 'You don't have to, you know?'

'My honour has been compromised,' said Wilderforce. 'I have no choice. As an officer and a gentleman, the regiment would expect no less from me than to accept this challenge.'

The man with the top hat summoned the other gentlemen to join them. Wilderforce took off his jacket, and passed it to his second, a much younger lower-ranking officer of the same regiment; 'He's right, you know,' whispered the younger man. 'The government passed a law making this tradition a crime. You may have to answer to the court, should you survive,' he advised.

'Simpson called my integrity into question, in front of the other men under my command,' said Wilderforce. 'That is reason enough.'

Simpson, a much older man than Wilderforce, now stood beside the man with the top hat. The older man took off his jacket and ceremoniously passed it to his second. 'I would have thought you would have run like the coward that I took you for,' he said, gruffly. 'At least you have shown some moral fortitude in your last hours.'

The man with the top hat opened the case in his possession. Inside the case were two duelling pistols. Each was loaded with a lead ball, and ready to fire. 'If you are ready, then each take a pistol, and stand back-to-back,' he said.

Wilderforce and Simpson each took a pistol from the case, and stood back-to- back. The man with the top hat, and the two seconds, walked a safe distance away.

'You will each take fifteen steps, on my count, turn and fire. Are you ready?'

Wilderforce and Simpson both nodded their assent. 'One…'

As the count was made, each made the requisite number of steps. It was as if time had stood still in this small forgotten corner of England. It was a time when an Englishman's word was his bond; when a man's honour was everything, and if it was brought into disrepute then the matter had to be dealt with accordingly in a civilised fashion.

As the count proceeded, Wilderforce thought of his regiment; he convinced himself that he was doing the honourable thing in confronting the perceived slight by Simpson. Although he had seen death many times in battle, his hand began to shake slightly, in anticipation of what was to come.

'Ten...'

Wilderforce thought of his wife. The thought of leaving her alone with their three-year-old daughter tore at his conscience, but made his resolve even firmer.

'Fourteen...'

This was it. *May god grant me courage in my hour of need.*

'Fifteen...'

Simpson and Wilderforce turned to face each other. They pointed their pistols, aimed carefully, and pulled the triggers. There was a flash from each pistol, and the acrid smell of spent gunpowder filled the air.

At first it was unclear if either Simpson *or* Wilderforce had been hit, until Wilderforce realised that blood was beginning to emerge from his waistcoat. 'I am stricken,' he declared, clutching his stomach. The blood now poured more freely between his fingers, and he could feel his senses begin to fade. He fell to the ground, and when he looked up, he could see his second looking over him, frantically trying to quell the ceaseless flow of blood.

'I'm afraid it looks bad, sir.'

Wilderforce looked the young man in the eye. It took all of his remaining energy to whisper: 'Tell them I died with honour.'

Tears began to grow in the young man's eyes. 'I will sir,' he said.

Wilderforce was dead.

Darkness…

She stood in the dock before her peers, accused of witchcraft. At fifteen years of age, she was one of the youngest to be accused of practising the dark arts. Unable to read or write, she was an easy target for those seeking retribution for perceived wrongs outside of their control. A farmer by the name of Jenkins had caught the girl stealing apples from his orchard. When he confronted the girl, he testified that she put a curse on him, which resulted in him contracting smallpox. The trial had been hastily convened in the courtroom in Lancaster, in the county of Lancashire, by prosecutor John Stevens, who was the local magistrate, as well as the local witch-finder. Stevens had produced several witnesses, including the defendant's younger sister, who testified that the accused was heard to curse Jenkins. It was said by her sister that a black cat that was nearby spoke in a foreign tongue with the accused. Her fate was sealed. Nobody spoke on behalf of the girl as they did not want to suffer the wrath of the court by association – not even her parents.

The evidence now complete, the judge asked the jury if they had reached a verdict. A middle-aged peasant stood up on behalf of the jury.

'We have, your honour.'

'What say you?'

'Guilty.'

The judge turned to the accused. 'Sarah Wilderforce, you have been found guilty of witchcraft by a court of your peers. In accordance with the law, as decreed by his Majesty, King James, you will be taken henceforth to Lancaster Castle to await your execution two days hence, when you will be taken to Gallows Hill, and hung until you be dead.' He turned to the two soldiers who were in attendance by the large oak door. 'Take her away.'

The two soldiers dragged Sarah to the enclosed cart which was waiting outside of the courtroom.

As she stood in the cart on her journey to Lancaster Castle, Sarah replayed the events of the trial. Her younger sister, Florence, with whom she had argued with recently, had enacted her revenge in the most gruesome way, by lying to the court and making false accusations against her. The farmer had lied too. Admittedly, she had taken an apple from the tree, but it was only because she was hungry, as her family were poor and couldn't afford the luxury of regular food on the table. She was a victim of cruel circumstance. She began to pray for her soul.

The cell in the castle was damp and dirty. Rats ran freely around the stone floor, looking for scraps to eat. Water slowly dripped down the walls. It was a miserable dark and dank place to be incarcerated. She did not deserve such an end to her short life, she thought. What hopes she had had for her future; perhaps marriage… children? All now just visions lost in the fog of injustice…

As Sarah stood on the gallows platform at Gallows Hill, there was a large crowd before her who believed her to be guilty of a crime for which she knew she was innocent. Many threw mouldy vegetables at her as the hangman placed a small canvas sack over her head. A noose was placed around her neck, and Sarah was pushed off the platform.

Darkness…

The sea raged like an angry god. Thiry and forty-foot waves persistently slammed against the sides of the five British warships that were in hot pursuit of the Spanish merchant ship; on its port and starboard sides were two heavily-armed galleons. In accordance with the blessing of Queen Elizabeth, the privateers were commissioned to board and plunder Spanish merchant ships, at their disposal, in order to swell the coffers of Her Majesty. Thus far the Queen and her entourage were pleased with the privateers' contribution to the royal household, and as long as she benefited from this practice, she would informally convey her acquiescence.

As the young man looked from his vantage point in the crow's nest, he could see that, under full sail, they were rapidly approaching their intended target. They would have to engage with the two galleons, within the hour, but they had overwhelming superiority in numbers which gave them the upper hand. The spray from the waves soaked through his brown doublet, cotton shirt and hide breeches.

'Mister Wilderforce!' came the cry from the Captain below.

'Yes, Captain?' replied the young man.

'What is the firepower of those warships?'

'Fourteen cannon a-piece, sir!'

'Very well!'

This was the third engagement that Wilderforce had experienced thus far. Despite only being nineteen years of age, he was now an old hand in sea warfare, since running away from home and becoming a cabin boy on board The Fortitude. The British warship had three masts at full sail, and was armed with twenty eight-pounder cannons.

A fellow able-bodied seaman, who stood beside Wilderforce was also scouring the seas; he was a much older man who had served over twenty years as a privateer. 'It'll not be long now, lad,' he said. He took a small bottle of rum from his pocket and handed it to the boy. 'For courage.'

Wilderforce declined the offer, knowing that he risked flogging if caught taking spirits just before a major engagement. Besides, he didn't need alcohol to quell his nerves, as he saw warfare as the great adventure. He picked up his musket and gripped it tightly. So far, he had been lucky. Each campaign had resulted in victory and the reward had been good. He had sent most of his pay to his grateful family in Plymouth, who were experiencing hard times during great upheaval due to plague and pestilence in the area.

The call from the Captain came: 'Man the cannons!'

Other senior ranked officers relayed the command, and the gunners opened the gun doors, and prepared the cannons for the oncoming battle. It was a manoeuvre that had been practised hundreds of times – failure to do so in a timely fashion would have meant severe repercussions for the gunners. Wilderforce and the elder crewman prepared their muskets in readiness for sniper duties against the enemy.

As The Fortitude came alongside the starboard flank of the lead galleon that was protecting the Spanish merchant ship, the order to open fire for the first cannon was given. The gunners instinctively knew that they had to fire when the ship was at the height of the swells. The first shot overreached it's intended target by quite a margin. The second cannon ploughed its shot through the upper hull of the galleon but it was still seaworthy. The four other British warships were now also in the fray, and the slaughter of the enemy began. The Spanish galleons, although vastly outgunned, began to retaliate with their own cannons. Soon the sea became a mist of burnt gunpowder, and the smoke from the smouldering masts of the Spanish galleon made it difficult for the men to breathe. A few Spanish sailors jumped into the sea to avoid being burned to death. The noise and chaos that ensued was an inferno that seemed as though it came from the very depth of the devil's lair. Wilderforce, and his fellow seaman, were close enough to the enemy's position that they began to open fire. The main target was the Spanish Captain – if they could dispatch him then the end would be near. It was as if the battle was happening in slow motion.

As Wilderforce was reloading his musket, which proved difficult in the heat of battle and the continuing storm, a shot from the enemy's cannon ripped through the mast, and threw the two men into the sea.

He held on tightly to a large piece of wood that floated beside him. As he looked up, he could see the huge ships before him which looked like sea monsters towering over him. Both The Fortitude and the Spanish galleon were in dire straits; each ship was on fire and in imminent danger of sinking. Wilderforce instinctively knew that his life was in jeopardy. He had never learned to swim. Others were now in the water, dead and dying. Screams from those afflicted by war filled the air.

Wilderforce felt for his legs but they were not there. He cried for his mother as the waves enveloped him. His grip on the wood faltered, and he found himself sinking below to his watery grave. As he looked up from his descent, he could see the flames that were once so bright begin slowly to dim, until they were no longer there.

Darkness…

Henry could hear muffled voices. Had he finally died and was now in hell? A strange soft pale light filled his eyes. He remembered those strange dreams that seemed so real. He must have fallen asleep, he thought, but he couldn't remember going to bed. He was walking down a street when the weather became stormy. That was the last thing that he remembered from that day. But the dreams… They were etched on his mind. He had a connection with each of them:

a name. How can that be possible? Is this what it is like to be dead, he wondered? The voices became louder. The light grew more intense.

'I think he's coming round,' said a voice. It was a female voice.

'Get the doctor,' said another. A young man's voice.

There was a long moment of quiet.

'Mister Wilderforce?' It was the voice of an older man.

'Hmm?'

'Mister Wilderforce. Can you hear me?'

'Hmm?'

Somebody lifted one of his eyelids and shone a light into his eye. The brightness hurt his senses, and Henry winced.

'He's coming round. Slowly,' said the older man, with conviction. 'Mister Wilderforce. Can you hear me?'

Henry slowly opened his eyes. Something was covering his mouth. Various tubes were in his arms. Am I being tortured, he wondered? His mind began to play tricks on him. Perhaps this was another dream, he thought. But it feels as real as all the others did. It took quite a while for him to realise that he was in a bed. A hospital bed. He looked directly at the man who was looking so closely at him.

'Who are you?' Henry managed to whisper.

'My name is Doctor Sully. Can you tell me your name?

Henry looked around the hospital ward. There were several nurses and doctors who were all looking at him. 'Henry... Henry Wilderforce,' he said.

'Henry,' said the doctor. You've been in a coma.'

'Have I?'

The doctor, who had a kind face, smiled and nodded. 'You've been in a coma for over six months...'

Henry continued his walks. He continued to think that life was strange. He never told anybody about his dreams while he was in an unconscious state. He had always kept himself to himself. That was just his way.

Besides… who would believe him?

The Man Who Made Them Laugh

Joe Mangle wanted to be a stand-up comedian for as long as he could remember. He was raised on a rich televisual diet of Billy Connolly, Steve Martin, Richard Pryor, Bill Hicks, Dave Allen, to name just a few of his all-time heroes. There was just one thing that always held him back: he wasn't funny.

Joe had tried everything to make people laugh. He did routines at comedy stores, pubs, clubs and holiday venues. He had worn costumes. He had paid somebody else to write his material. He had entered talent contests, but never won. He'd even resorted to physical comedy which went down like a lead balloon. Nothing he did, it seems, would make the audience howl with unrestricted merriment. But Joe was a stickler... If it was the last thing he did, he would make them all laugh.

He'd told himself years ago that one day he would be able to give up his job as a postal delivery man, and live in the lap of luxury that a comedian of his calibre deserved. But time marched on, and he had been retired now for ten years, having spent over forty years delivering mail. That ship had sailed. And in the blink of an eye too. He still lived in a one-bedroom flat in Ulverston, Lancashire, that he had bought when he was about thirty.

Joe was an optimist. Although he was now over seventy years of age, he still felt that if he had the right material, and the right venue, he could have them rolling in the aisles.

As Joe closed the bathroom cabinet that held a myriad of pills, he looked in the mirror and saw an old man looking back at him. It was a kind face, full of wrinkles; blue eyes that had seen a lifetime of promise pass him by; not much hair left, but it was tidy. Where did time go? He'd been so busy trying to make it as a comedian, as well as maintaining a regular job, that he never made time for anybody else in his life. Was that selfish, he wondered, or simply sad? Had he wasted his life? What would he be remembered for?

After he had brushed his teeth, he switched off the bathroom light, and climbed into bed. It took a long time for him to get to sleep, as he was thinking of the past, and trying to reconcile the future.

Joe was backstage, pacing back and forth. He wore his best black suit with a bright orange shirt, and glossy black shoes. In a few minutes it would be his turn to perform. Despite all those years of hopelessly pursuing a career as a stand-up comedian, he still felt the horror of stage fright before he went on. He had played here at the Beluga Comedy Store in Blackpool for more years than he cared to remember. It was an open mic evening for budding comedians, and he had five minutes to make the audience, which consisted of about fifteen people, laugh. Sometimes the MC would cut his act short, which Joe found very humiliating, but it never deterred him. He would come back like the proverbial comic boomerang that he was.

The act before Joe, had the audience warmed up, and they laughed in all the right places before he left the stage. The MC, who was a chubby middle-aged man wearing a loud suit, took the microphone from the last act, and introduced Joe to the audience.

'Ladies and gentlemen, please give it up for an old act… and I do mean *old*. He's been around the block a few times. He's a regular at the Beluga. Give it up for… Joe Mangle!'

There were a few polite claps from the audience. Most of them had seen Joe perform before and knew what they were in for.

Joe came out onto the stage, and took the microphone from the MC. 'Thank you for that rapturous welcome,' he said. 'I know what you're thinking: Since when did Brad Pitt start doing stand-up?' One lady coughed, and a young couple started talking to each other... loudly. Joe plodded on despite this minor setback. He was almost immune to the reality of live performance, even if it *was* for just five minutes. 'What *is* it with those supermarket queues? I bought a box of eggs the other day; by the time I got to the checkout, they'd *hatched*.' Joe looked around the audience. Nothing. He'd half expected tumbleweed to swirl across the stage. 'Seriously though...' Joe tried smiling at them to lighten his load, but it came out like the last desperate expression of a condemned man. 'I was driving on the M25 to a wedding the other week; the traffic was so bad that by the time I got to the ceremony they had already *divorced*.' One lady in the audience started to choke on a peanut, and somebody else began conducting the Heimlich manoeuvre on her. Joe was used to dying on stage, but he had never lost an audience member before. Time to bring out the big guns. 'I went to see the doctor last week. He said: The good news is that you've got the body of an eighteen-year-old. I said: That's brilliant. What's the bad news? He said: You're not a dog.' The audience looked at him as though he had just broken wind. Joe was determined to salvage some pride. 'If you think that was funny wait til you hear *this*... I took up yoga a couple of weeks ago. The instructor said: Before long you will be so flexible that you'll be able to bend over backwards and walk like a crab, which will impress the women. I said: Sounds a bit shellfish.' There was an audible moan from the audience. He was fading fast. 'A friend of mine tried this new diet to lose weight. It's called the eat all you want and never mind the consequences diet. It's amazing. He lost thirteen stone. Well... he did after they cremated him.' He looked at faces that all had the same expression of bewilderment. Woke, he concluded.

The MC rushed back onto the stage and hastily grabbed the microphone from Joe.

'Let's hear it for Joe Mangle, ladies and gentlemen!'

Joe gave a begrudged wave to the audience, who gave a faint ripple of applause, and then he made his exit towards the bar. He needed a drink…

After a few pints of beer, Joe reflected on the evening. Maybe it was time to finally admit defeat, he thought. It suddenly dawned on him that he had spent his entire adult life trying to make people laugh – and had failed miserably. A worthy endeavour, he concluded, but nonetheless…

'I caught your act.'

Joe looked around. It was the deep voice of an elderly man, like him, and the accent had a slight American twang to it. The man was seated at the bar further down from Joe. He was a slim man, thinning salt and pepper hair, clean-shaven, and he looked worldly wise. He wore a tweed suit with a white shirt, woollen tie and brown shoes. 'You have my deepest sympathy,' said Joe. 'Do I know you? You look vaguely familiar.'

'We've never met, as far as I know.'

It seemed odd to Joe that the man wasn't drinking. 'What did you think?' The man looked at Joe quizzically. 'Of the act, I mean.'

'I've seen better,' he replied, matter-of-factly. 'As I'm sure have you.'

Joe had to concede that he had. 'Can I get you a drink…?'

'Arthur,' the man replied. 'But you can call me Stan. I don't drink anymore. It's not good for you, you know.'

Joe was intrigued by this mysterious person. 'I only drink when the act doesn't go well,' he said.

'You must be an alcoholic.'

Joe laughed. He was beginning to warm to Stan. 'Are you a comedian?'

'Of sorts. Long time ago. Way back when.'

'Are you from here?'

'I was born not far away. Did a lot of travelling, but my roots are always here.'

Joe moved closer to Stan. 'What made you give it up? Showbusiness, I mean.'

'I was part of a double act. He died, and I was left on my own.'

'Sorry to hear that. That must have been hard.'

'It was. It was like losing a brother, I suppose.'

Stan was lost in thought for a moment.

'Do you have any tips for me?' asked Joe.

Stan nodded. 'Be yourself,' he said, seriously. 'Don't try to be a comedian.'

Joe considered Stan's words. It was simple advice, but effective. It got to the heart of everything that he realised was wrong with his act. 'Nobody's ever said that to me. You're right. But it's easier said than done.'

'Of course,' replied Stan. 'It takes a lot of courage to just be yourself. But the audience knows a faker when it sees one. They can smell it. The best comedians in the business are mostly themselves. Of course, you need good material but if it's not honest it won't travel.'

'I could have done with your wisdom thirty years ago,' said Joe.

'It's never too late. There have been lots of comedy acts that have found success in their later years. Better late than never.'

Joe finished his pint, and then motioned to the bartender. 'Same again, please Dave.' He looked to Stan. 'Are you sure you don't want a drink?'

Stan shook his head. 'I'm alright thanks.'

Dave began pouring Joe's drink and then looked to him with concern. 'Are you okay, Joe?'

'Never felt better thanks.'

Dave passed the pint of beer to Joe, took his payment, and then attended to another customer further down the bar.

'What brings you to the Beluga, Stan?' asked Joe.

'We worked here years ago. Of course it was different back then. It was more variety acts. Vaudeville, you might say.'

This guy is older than he looks, thought Joe. 'Do you miss those days?'

Stan smiled wistfully. 'The world was our oyster. It was a lot more innocent back then, in a way, but good comedy will always stand the test of time.'

'I agree,' said Joe. But it's knowing what makes an audience laugh. I still haven't found that magic ingredient... I'm beginning to think I never will.'

'Perhaps you're trying too hard?'

'How do you mean?'

There was a thoughtful pause.

'What is it in your life that you find a challenge?' asked Stan.

'Oh, that's easy... Getting old.'

Stan smiled at Joe. It was almost like an epiphany. 'That might just be your salvation. It's something that the audience can relate to. Every family has grandparents who struggle with infirmity. You could build a repertoire around it. What are your own experiences with getting old?'

Joe thought long and hard. 'Where do I start...? Back ache. Forgetting where I put my keys. Calling people by the wrong name. Seeing other people that I used to know die from some age-related illness. People giving up their seats on a packed bus. Getting out of breath when walking to the shops. Becoming a grumpy old git for no reason whatsoever. Living in the past. Realising that my time on this planet is limited.... Need I go on?'

'Comedy gold.'

'Really? Wouldn't I be in danger of alienating the audience?'

'Quite the opposite,' said Stan. 'They will empathise with you, if you play your cards right. It's relatable. They know exactly what you're going through because they have somebody in their midst who is experiencing the same. Everybody will get old, and everybody will die. It's a fact of life you can't escape from.'

Joe finished his drink. 'I think you might have something there,' he said. 'You know what? I'll take your advice.' He got up to leave. 'I'll make them all laugh if it's the last thing I do.'

'Careful what you wish for.'

'I'd best be off. Lovely to meet you, Stan. And thanks again.' They shook hands. As Joe was about to leave, he turned to Stan. 'What's your last name, by the way?'

'Jefferson.'

'I hope you'll be here next time I perform at the Beluga?'

'You can count on it,' said Stan. 'I find myself drawn to this place.'

As Joe left the Beluga, and began walking to his bus stop, he thought about Stan's suggestion. Not bad, he thought. He began formulating ideas for his next comedy gig. It just might work... Nice bloke, that Stan. He looked very familiar, but Joe couldn't quite place him. Seemed to know a lot about comedy. And he was in a double act... But Joe didn't recognise the name Jefferson. It'll come to me, he thought.

A few weeks passed, and Joe had worked out a routine that sounded funny in his head, but the proof of the pudding was in the eating. Meeting Stan that night might just be the boost that he needed to finally make them laugh. He counted himself very lucky that he happened to meet someone who had a successful career in comedy, and was able to give him a few pointers. He decided to return to the Beluga to try out his new material on the audience.

Joe stood in the wings waiting to go on. It was a packed house for a change. Stage fright still affected him, and he thought he was going to throw up, but he managed to keep his nerve as the MC announced him.

'Ladies and gentleman, the next act is an old favourite. In fact, he's so old that Winston Churchill once dubbed him the next best thing since Charlie Chaplin. Please give it up for the one and only, our very own... Joe Mangle!'

Joe took the microphone from the MC and acknowledged the reluctant applause from the audience. 'Thank you very much. You're very kind. You know, it's not much fun getting old. It only seems like five minutes ago I was in diapers... Oh... that *was* five minutes ago.' There were a few laughs which Joe found encouraging. 'People often ask me: What's it like to be your age? And I always say: Pardon?' The audience were starting to warm to him. 'The worst part of ageing, without question, is forgetfulness... not sure where I'm going with that...' Now they were like a fish on a hook. Joe was enjoying himself. 'I was in the local library the other day. I asked the librarian: Do you have any books on the changing perception by the political elite towards an ageing population? And she said: This is a laundrette, you dickhead.' Lots of laughs. 'Charming... You see, people don't realise what you have to endure when you've reached a certain age. They think we've got it easy. Take bowel movements... it's like pushing a melon through the eye of a needle!' The audience erupted. 'I used to be able to do fifty push ups, and not break a sweat. These days I have to have a lie down after taking the lid off a jam jar. It's not fair...' He was hitting the mark. The audience was in the palm of his hand. 'And don't talk to me about libido... The only thing that rises these days is my temperature...' As the audience laughed in unison, Joe could see in the corner of his eye that Stan was standing in the wings, laughing along with them. He gave the thumbs-up sign to Joe. That was all Joe needed. He must be doing something right. 'I still keep in touch with all my old friends, though... I read the obituary column every day...' Joe smiled as the audience lapped it up. 'It's good to keep in touch... They say a fine wine matures with age. Let's see... I have back ache, haemorrhoids, incontinence, forgetfulness, blurred vision, deafness, trouble sleeping, trouble walking, I call people by their wrong name, I'm grumpy for no reason, and I live in the past... That's a fine whine, I suppose...' Some of the audience clapped. 'I'll let you think about that for a while...' Joe grinned. 'No... getting old isn't always so bad. You can break wind in public and people will say: Aw, bless him. You try it and they'll punch you in the face... You can create a queue a mile long behind you at the supermarket checkout, while you slowly and deliberately count out your loose change... That's always a good one. It's good to have a hobby... You can get away with a lot when you're old... When somebody asks me: What was it like in your day? I tell them: We had wars that never seemed to end. Jobs that paid a pittance. There were food shortages. Strikes left, right, and centre. Riots in the streets. Outbreaks of disease. Pollution. Public telephones. You had to wait for the television to warm up before it came on. And they were so big they took up half the room. Toilet rolls were made of greaseproof paper. Greaseproof *paper*, would you believe... It was like trying to pick up a fried egg with your fingers...' Some in the audience laughed hysterically. 'God, I miss those days...' Joe smiled mischievously. 'I'm Joe Mangle, and you've been great. Goodnight!' The audience went wild and gave Joe a standing ovation. Joe bowed, and soaked up the adulation. He *did* it. He made them laugh. He felt on top of the world. The wait had been worth it.

The MC came on stage and took the microphone from Joe. 'Joe Mangle, ladies and gentlemen!'

Joe took an extra bow, and then reluctantly left the stage.

It was a still dark night. There was very little traffic on the roads, and the air was refreshingly cool, as Joe began his long walk to his bus stop. He was reliving the best night of his life in his head. Each joke that he had told hit home with the audience. It was unbelievable. Nothing had ever felt this satisfying.

'Mind if I join you?'

Joe looked behind him. Stan's voice was unmistakeable. He stopped walking and happily let Stan catch up.

'Of course,' said Joe.

They walked together side-by-side. An unspoken bond existed between them as they continued to walk.

It was Stan who finally broke the silence. 'I enjoyed your act, Joe. You were very funny.'

'It's all thanks to you, Stan. If you hadn't given me that encouragement, I would never have changed my act.'

'I could tell how important it was to you.'

Joe glanced at Stan. 'How?' he said.

'Oh… I've been around the block a few times. I felt much the same in my day. Comedy is in our blood.'

'It all came together this evening. I can't thank you enough…'

Stan could suddenly sense a feeling of melancholy in Joe's tone and change of expression – instinctively, he expected it. 'It was in you all the time, Joe. You just had to find it,' he said, gently.

They reached the bus stop, and sat down beside each other on the small bench. A silent impenetrable connection existed between them.

'This will be my last gig,' declared Joe, solemnly. Stan listened intently without interruption. 'You see, Stan... I'm not a well man.' Joe closed his eyes in calm resignation. 'My doctor thinks another three months at best...'

'I know...'

Joe opened his eyes. 'But how could you poss-'

As Joe looked to his side, he realised that he was now conspicuously alone. Stan was nowhere to be seen. He sat in quiet contemplation, trying to make sense of it all, and concluded that there wasn't any. Life, as in death, is a mystery and always will be, he concluded. Was Stan real? Perhaps he was a ghost, or his guardian angel?

On the bus journey home, Joe looked out of the window, lost in thoughts of his past life and his future. Despite the challenges he had faced, it had been a worthwhile journey. He wasn't scared of dying. Joe had finally made them laugh, and the satisfaction that he felt inside made him smile.

The Doppelganger

It was a balmy summer's evening as Geoffrey Pinkleton and his partner, Olivia Minster, leisurely strolled through the park in Greenwich, London, with their dog Trace, a five-year-old white Scottish Terrier that loved everybody, and had a zest for life that was infectious. The happy couple, in their early thirties, lived just a stone's throw away from the park, in a small mid-terraced Victorian house.

Tall and athletic, with dark curly hair, Geoffrey was quite the contrast to Olivia, who was slight in stature, pretty, and with long blonde hair tied efficiently at the back.

It was a beautiful spacious park that had long meandering paths interspersed with ancient trees and undulating fields of green. Geoffrey and Olivia often took long evening walks together, as it melted away the inevitable stress that came from their chosen professions: Geoffrey ran an online training course in computer programming, from home, and Olivia was a mathematics teacher at the local Academy school.

There were a lot of people, young and old, milling around them in all directions who were also enjoying the park, and Trace had quite a time pulling against his lead trying to meet and greet as many people as he could. Geoffrey had to rein the dog back now and then to prevent him from being a nuisance to anyone who might not be so enamoured with his enthusiasm.

'It's lovely here, isn't it?' declared Olivia. 'We're very lucky to have this on our doorstep.'

Geoffrey nodded his agreement. 'Sometimes I have to pinch myself.' He reached out to Olivia who instinctively took his hand.

'I wonder if we'll still be doing this in our old age?'

Geoffrey smiled, mischievously. 'You might have to carry me.'

'Maybe I'll have a toyboy by then.'

'Charming.'

They stopped in their tracks and exchanged a lingering kiss.

It was Olivia who spoke first as they continued their walk. 'I suppose I can put up with you for a bit.'

'Good to know.'

Approaching them, from the opposite direction, was a familiar face. It was one of their closest friends, Alec Delaney, who was walking his elderly Alsatian dog, Misty. Alec, a similar age to Geoffrey, was a tall redhead, scruffily dressed in ripped jeans and t-shirt.

'Greetings, you two,' said Alec. 'Not sure I should be talking to you, Geoffrey!'

'Good to see you, Alec,' said Olivia.

'Why shouldn't you be talking to *me*?' enquired Geoffrey, who was more than a little put out. 'What did *I* do?'

Trace and Misty reacquainted themselves by sniffing each other the way dogs do.

'I was walking down the High Street three days ago, and you completely blanked me. You walked right past me as though I didn't exist. I called after you, but you seemed to be in another world.'

'Really…? Doesn't sound like me. It's not like I hardly know you – we were schoolmates, after all.'

'Exactly. I suppose I can let you off, but it was a bit of a surprise. Maybe you had a lot on your plate?'

Olivia turned to Geoffrey. 'You have been a little stressed at home lately. Your workload is not what it was.'

'Even so…,' said Geoffrey. He turned to Alec. 'Sorry about that… I had no idea…'

'You could buy me a pint to make up for it, if you like? I'll be down The Dog and Whistle. I'm meeting up with Jim Crossley at eight. You remember Jim?'

'Of course. We played football in the same local team,' said Geoffrey. He turned to Olivia. 'Are you up for a beer?'

Olivia shook her head. 'I've got some papers to mark later. But you go ahead. Sounds like you owe Alec a drink.'

Geoffrey turned to Alec. 'Okay. I'll see you down The Dog and Whistle a bit later on.'

Alec bid his farewell, and went on his way, leaving Geoffrey feeling perplexed. 'That was weird,' he said. 'I don't even remember being *in* the High Street three days ago. Think he might be losing it.'

'We're all a little preoccupied sometimes. Happens to the best of us. Even you.'

'I suppose you're right.'

They continued on in their walk, oblivious to the dark events that would later unfold.

As Geoffrey entered the Dog and Whistle, he had to scour the pub for Alec and Jim. There were a lot of noisy customers at the bar. There was a large group of young people who were celebrating something or other. He spotted his friends who were propping up the far end of the bar, and made his way towards them.

'Hi guys,' he said, as he approached Alec and Jim. 'Can I get you a refill?'

'Don't mind if I do,' said Alec. 'Lager.'

'Hi Geoff,' said Jim. 'Long time no see.' He shook hands with Geoffrey. 'Guinness please.'

Geoffrey noticed that Jim's salt-and-pepper hair was much longer than when he had last seen him, and he now sported a scraggly beard, and looked a bit dishevelled in old jeans and a t-shirt that had seen better days. He managed to get the attention of Paul, the elderly barman and owner of the pub, and ordered drinks. 'Two pints of lager and a pint of Guinness please, Paul'

'Twice in one week?' said Paul. 'Not like you?'

Paul began pouring the drinks.

'What do you mean? I haven't been in here for weeks.'

Paul looked confused, and a little embarrassed. 'Oh… My mistake, I guess.'

Geoffrey paid for the drinks and took them to his friends. He sat down beside them. 'Cheers chaps. I feel like I need this…'

'Is your other half giving you grief?' asked Jim.

Geoffrey shook his head. 'Far from it. It's nothing, I don't suppose… How's things with you?'

Jim looked sheepish. 'I got divorced.'

'Oh shit. I had no idea. I'm so sorry.'

Jim shrugged his shoulders. 'Can't be helped. Our relationship was always a bit… rocky.'

'He's young free and single again,' said Alec, consolingly.

'It was finalised a couple of weeks ago,' said Jim. 'She's still got some of my stuff.'

'Where are you staying?' asked Geoffrey.

'In a flat above a bookmaker's. It will do for now until I can afford something better. She got the house and custody of Wendy, which I agreed to.'

'How old is Wendy now?' asked Alec.

'Three.'

'Do you still have your job as an heir hunter?' asked Geoffrey.

'Probate researcher,' corrected Jim. 'They've given me a few weeks off to sort myself out. Compassionate leave.'

Geoffrey raised his glass to Jim. 'Good luck to you. I'm sure things will work out, in the long run.'

Alec nodded, sympathetically. 'Plenty more fish in the sea.'

Jim smiled, reluctantly. 'Knowing my luck it will be a shark…'

The next day, Geoffrey and Olivia were at home, sat on the settee in the lounge, watching a late-night film. Trace was contentedly sat on Olivia's lap, sleeping peacefully, when the doorbell rang.

'Who the hell is that at this time of night?' said Geoffrey.

Trace woke with a start, jumped off Olivia's lap, and barked at the door.

'You'd best see who it is. Might be important,' said Olivia.

Geoffrey opened the front door. Standing before him was a grey-haired middle-aged man, wearing a dark overcoat; beside him was a younger woman, probably in her mid-thirties, auburn-haired, wearing a light raincoat. Behind them was a young male uniformed police officer.

The man spoke first. 'Geoffrey Pinkleton?'

'Yes?'

'I'm Detective Inspector Jennings, and this is my colleague Detective Inspector Simms, as well as PC Kendall. Would you mind if we came in and had a word, please?'

Geoffrey looked at the three police officers with some trepidation. 'What's it concerning?'

Olivia called out from the lounge. 'Who is it Geoff?'

'The police. They want to come in for a chat.'

Olivia joined Geoffrey at the door, and confronted the two police officers. 'What do you want?'

It was Simms who spoke first. 'It might be better if we can talk inside, if that's okay?'

Olivia picked up Trace, who by now had stopped barking. 'I suppose you'd better come in,' she said, reluctantly.

The three police officers came into the house, and stood in the lounge. Geoffrey switched off the television, and stood beside Olivia.

'What's going on?' demanded Geoffrey.

It was Jennings who spoke first. 'We're conducting an investigation into an assault that occurred yesterday evening. An elderly gentleman was attacked in his home, and is currently in hospital, receiving medical attention.'

'And what the hell does that have to do with us?' said Geoffrey, somewhat irritated.

Simms gave an explanation: 'A man fitting your description was seen leaving the premises in question, therefore we need you to come to the station to answer some questions that we have in relation to this crime.'

Jennings signalled to Kendall, who approached Geoffrey, with a set of handcuffs.

'You are being arrested under suspicion of Grievous Bodily Harm,' Kendall said. He asked Geoffrey to put his hands behind his back, and he then clasped the handcuffs on his wrists. 'You do not have to say anything, but it may harm your defence if you do not mention when questioned something which you later rely on in court.'

Geoffrey was dumbfounded. 'This is ridiculous!' he shouted. You're making a huge mistake. I will sue the lot of you.'

'We're just doing our job,' said Simms. 'You'll have a chance to explain your side of the story down at the station.' They began to lead Geoffrey out of the house.

Olivia began to sob, uncontrollably. 'Geoffrey!'

Geoffrey turned to Olivia as he was being led out. 'Don't worry, Olivia, I'll be back before long. I've done nothing wrong!'

Geoffrey was taken to a police car that was waiting outside the house, and driven off. Olivia stood at the doorway, in floods of tears, not quite believing what had just taken place.

At the police station, Geoffrey had his handcuffs removed, and was led to the front desk, where a sergeant took his personal details, and formally explained why he was in custody. He had his mobile phone taken from him and he was then taken to a holding cell – he had to remove his shoes and belt outside before entering. The door was slammed shut behind him.

It was a small cell with peeling yellow paint on the walls. A hard mattress, on a bench, encased in a plastic sheet, was at the side of the cell. There were a number of flies embedded in a cobweb in one corner of the ceiling. A CCTV camera was on a bracket in another corner of the ceiling, pointed downwards.

Geoffrey sat on the hard mattress, and despairingly held his head in his hands. An hour went by when PC Kendall opened his cell and asked Geoffrey to accompany him to another room where his fingerprints, photograph, and a swab sample of his saliva, were taken for their records. He was then taken back to his cell pending an official interview.

Olivia was in a state of limbo; she sat at the table, staring blankly ahead not wanting to believe what had taken place, thinking that Geoffrey would be returning at any moment now. It was hard to comprehend that he had been arrested by the police. She couldn't eat or drink, and replayed the evening's events over and over in her mind. What could she do…? Nothing… It was then that the doorbell rang. Her heart was racing. Trace ran to the door and barked loudly. Olivia assumed it would be Geoffrey – that it had all been a terrible mistake and that all was well again, but when she opened it there were three young police officers who showed their ID badges and explained that they had a search warrant to the premises and would be removing any items of interest concerning the assault. They said it was a matter of routine in this type of situation, and that the items would be returned in due course upon further review. During the next hour, the three police officers removed Geoffrey's laptop, various documents and some of Geoffrey's clothes as well as a pair of his shoes. They left swiftly once they were satisfied that they had taken what was necessary, leaving Olivia feeling numb.

Back at the police station, Geoffrey was being formally interviewed in a small enclosed room, by DI Jennings and DI Simms. Each police officer held notepads, and made notes as the interview progressed. A few upturned photographs were on the table, beside Simms.

'Are you sure that you don't want legal representation, Mister Pinkleton?' asked Jennings.

'I've done nothing wrong,' replied Geoffrey. 'I have nothing to hide.'

'Have you ever been in trouble with the law, Mister Pinkleton?' asked Simms.

'No.'

'That's not entirely true, is it?' stated Jennings. He looked through his notepad for details. 'You were arrested whilst driving under the influence. Isn't that correct?'

'I'd forgotten about that. I was barely in my twenties.'

'And yet you were arrested, lost six points off your licence, as well as receiving a fixed penalty notice?' reminded Simms.

'As I said. I forgot.'

Jennings looked agitated. 'If you're prepared to lie about that, then what else are you prepared to lie about?'

'It was a long time ago.'

'What type of work do you do, Mister Pinkleton?' asked Simms.

'I teach computer programming online.'

'And does it pay well?'

Geoffrey looked sheepish. 'It used to. The demand has tailed off quite a bit, that's for sure.'

'So, you've been having some financial problems?' asked Jennings.

'I'm certainly not wealthy if that's what you mean?'

Jennings allowed a poignant pause before adding: 'Interesting… We are working on the assumption that it was a robbery that went wrong.'

'Oh, come on! I'm not a crook!'

Simms turned over one of the photographs, and placed it in front of Geoffrey. 'This is one of the CCTV images taken from one of the victim's neighbours. Would you take a look?'

Geoffrey looked at the photograph; although grainy and dark, the figure walking away did look alarmingly like him. 'I'll admit that does look like me, but it's out of focus. It could be anyone,' he said, defensively.

Jennings decided to turn up the heat. Where were you on the night in question?'

'I was down the Dog and Whistle with two of my friends. Alec Delaney and Jim Crossley.'

'And they'll be able to corroborate that?' asked Simms.

'Of course.'

'What time did you leave the pub, Mister Pinkleton?' asked Jennings.

'Just before ten, I think.'

Simms looked with concern to Jennings, and then back to Geoffrey. 'The assault took place at approximately ten o'clock that evening,' she said. 'Where did you go after leaving the pub?'

'I went home, of course.'

'The victim's house is just a few blocks from the pub, Mister Pinkleton,' said Jennings. 'Perhaps you paid him a visit on your way home?'

'Mister Grainger is in a critical condition in hospital,' said Simms. 'The intruder's fingerprints were on the assault weapon.'

Jennings decided to up the ante. 'If they match yours, you are looking at a long stretch in prison.'

'It will be easier on you if you tell us what happened,' insisted Simms.

Geoffrey felt sick. 'I *told* you… I went home. You should be out there looking for the *real* culprit. Not wasting your time on *me*.'

Simms turned over another photograph, and laid it before Geoffrey; it was an image of Mister Grainger showing an injury to his head that Geoffrey would never forget. 'He's an old man, Mister Pinkleton. Blunt force trauma to the head can be devastating to an elderly person. If he dies…' Simms let her silence speak volumes.

'That poor man,' said Geoffrey, solemnly. 'It wasn't me. I don't know how many times I need to tell you, but I would never do anything like *that*, I assure you.'

'You'd be surprised how many times we hear that,' said Simms.

Jennings called for a break in the proceedings. The two police officers left the interview room leaving Geoffrey alone with his thoughts. How could this be happening, he wondered? He'd seen so many programmes on television where the police had detained the wrong man. Once they've made up their minds that they have the guilty party they don't let up. He looked up to the ceiling. The spider was busily encasing a live victim before he would eventually devour it. He knew how that poor fly felt…

A half hour passed. DI Jennings and DI Simms re-entered the room. Each of the police officers had a serious look upon their face.

It was Jennings who spoke first. 'Well, Mister Pinkleton, you're free to go, for now. The fingerprints on the assault weapon didn't match yours.'

Geoffrey, who by this time was exhausted, stood up. 'Perhaps now you can find the *real* perpetrator,' he said. 'I've been here for over five hours. That's five hours you've wasted when you could have been looking elsewhere.'

'We were just doing our job, Mister Pinkleton,' replied Simms.

Jennings added, 'We would be neglecting our duty if we didn't act upon information received. You must understand that?'

'I just want to go home. Please return my mobile.'

'In due course,' said Jennings. 'As with your laptop. As soon as forensics have completed their analysis, we will return your property.'

Geoffrey was incensed. 'You've also got my laptop? I need that for my work!'

'As I said, we will return your property in due course.'

'This is outrageous.'

Simms said, 'It's standard procedure, I assure you.'

Geoffrey was led out of the police station, and began the long walk home.

As Geoffrey walked through the dark empty streets to his home, he relived the events of the day in his mind's eye. Seeing those police officers when he opened his front door... It was all downhill from there. He felt violated. How could this happen to an innocent person? How many others had been detained in this way? Admittedly, when they showed him the CCTV image of the suspect, it did look remarkably like him. It's said that everyone throughout the world has a doppelganger – perhaps he had one that was too close for comfort?

It was nearly three o'clock in the morning when Geoffrey let himself in the front door of his house. It had been a long day. A day unlike any other. He was fondly greeted by Trace, who wagged his tail incessantly. Geoffrey picked up his dog, and was licked for all he was worth. He was grateful. It made him feel human again, instead of just a slab of meat. He saw Olivia, slumped at the table, fast asleep. He felt so guilty that events outside of his control had put her through all of this. She deserved better. He gently roused her, and as soon as she realised that he was back, she instinctively stood up and embraced him. Through tearful eyes they kissed. It had easily been the worst day of their lives. Their relief was immense.

'I'm exhausted,' sighed Geoffrey, wearily.

'What happened?'

'Mistaken identity.'

Olivia's tired smiling eyes said it all. 'Let's go to bed.'

'That's the best thing I've heard all day…'

They decided to put all that happened behind them, as best they could, and write it off as a day to forget.

A week passed before events would take an unexpected turn.

Geoffrey, Olivia, Alec and Jim were sat at the bar in the Dog and Whistle, enjoying a late evening drink, and engaged in friendly banter.

'So, what was it like?' asked Alec to Geoffrey.

'What was *what* like?'

'Being a jailbird.'

'I'm trying hard to forget. It was undoubtedly the worst experience of my life. Thanks for reminding me.'

Olivia placed a consoling hand on Geoffrey's leg.

Alec smiled mischievously. 'That's what friends are for.'

Jim looked puzzled. 'I don't get it. Why would they think *you* did it?'

'Because there's somebody out there that looks like me. You should have seen the CCTV image – he was a dead ringer.'

'What happened to the old man?' asked Alec.

'As far as I know he's still in hospital. Poor bastard. He was beaten up pretty badly.'

Olivia shrugged as though feeling a sudden chill. 'There are some sick people in this world.'

'Maybe he was a druggie. Off his nut,' said Alec, dismissively.

Jim nodded. 'They'd rob their old granny for a fix.'

There was a lull in the conversation.

Olivia decided to change the subject. 'How much longer will you be off work?' she asked Jim.

'Another couple of weeks.'

'What is it you do, exactly?'

'People often die without leaving a will. It's my job to determine if the deceased had any family that are due a share of their estate. We check births, deaths, historical records such as the census to locate them. Quite often it unearths relations who didn't even know that they had a connection with the deceased. Sometimes the amounts are astronomical, but more often than not it's just a few hundred quid.'

'Sounds more interesting than teaching haughty teenagers the merits of algebra,' said Olivia, derisively.

'It's like all jobs really. It has its highs and lows. But it can be quite satisfying when you've located somebody out of the blue.'

'Sounds far too technical,' said Alec. 'I'll stick to boring old accounting any day.'

'You are all lucky. They've kept my laptop so I can't even earn an honest crust at the moment.'

'I'm sure you'll get it back before long,' said Olivia.

Jim got off his stool and approached the bar. 'Time for a refill.' He looked to the others. 'One for the road?'

'Only if you insist,' said Geoffrey. As Jim was ordering the drinks, Geoffrey could see out of the corner of his eye three people approaching their area – and they seemed to be in a hurry. One of them wore a policeman's uniform. As they approached, Geoffrey recognised them: it was DI Jennings, DI Simms, and PC Kendall. 'Oh my god, look who's turned up.'

They all turned round to face the police officers who were now suddenly beside them.

Olivia spoke first with some venom in her voice: 'Have you got nothing better to do than bother innocent people?'

'This has to be a mistake,' insisted Alec.

PC Kendall spoke first. 'Geoffrey Pinkleton, I'm arresting you on the charge of Grievous Bodily Harm.' As he took out his handcuffs and began attaching them to Geoffrey's wrists, he added, 'You do not have to say anything, but it may harm your defence if you do not mention when questioned something which you later rely on in court.'

'What the hell?' shouted Geoffrey. 'This has to be a frame up.'

Jennings said, 'You left your DNA at the scene of the crime. That was careless of you, Mister Pinkleton.'

'Bastards,' declared Olivia, tearfully. 'You've made one enormous cock up.'

As Geoffrey was led away, Simms turned around briefly. 'DNA doesn't lie, I'm afraid.'

Alec and Jim tried to console Olivia, who was shaking with emotion.

'It will be okay,' said Alec, trying to remain calm in the face of adversity. 'Mistakes happen. We all know that Geoffrey wouldn't hurt a fly, let alone beat up an innocent old man.'

Jim nodded in agreement. 'There's something that doesn't add up about all of this.' He put his hand comfortingly on Olivia's. 'Olivia, I need you to give me certain information about Geoff. It's a long shot but I think I may be able to help...'

Several days passed. Jim sat at his desk rigorously viewing details on his laptop that he had unearthed from various sources regarding Geoffrey. With the information that he had gleaned from Olivia, and subsequent to talking to Geoffrey's parents, he was able to establish facts that he hoped may eventually help his friend, who was currently languishing in prison awaiting a trial date. He managed to utilise his skills that he had established from working as a probate researcher, and had accessed systems online that only a very few were allowed entry to. There was one particular person that he needed to track down who might be able to shed some light on his friend's dilemma...

Olivia was in a permanent state of disbelief. As she sat at the table mulling the events of the past in her head, she felt numb. How was it possible that Geoff's DNA was found at the scene of a crime? Was it a stitch-up by the police? It wouldn't be the first time, and undoubtedly there have been corrupt officers in the past who have been known to bend the law in order to make themselves look good. Time seemed to stand still. She wasn't able to work, and she couldn't think straight. It was like being in a bad dream and she wasn't able to wake up. Without her dog Trace for company, she would have gone mad. She hoped and prayed that Geoff's friend Jim would be able to shed some light on all of this darkness.

Jim parked his car on the side road, got out, and approached the small terraced house with some trepidation; it was in a run-down area in East London that had probably been neglected for years. Rubbish had accumulated in the front garden over time, and cats were busily chasing each other in between old discarded furniture that had seen better days. Tentatively he rang the doorbell. He heard the sound of somebody walking down some wooden stairs. When the door opened, Jim faced a lady who looked about fifty years of age; she was fairly tall, had long dark curly hair, wore a blue dress, and had a kind face.

'Yes?' she said, rather curtly. 'If you're selling something, you're wasting your time.'

'Are you Angela Pritchy?' he asked.

'Who wants to know?'

Jim felt a little self-conscious but persevered. 'My name is Jim Crossley. You don't know me, but I'm a friend of Geoffrey Pinkleton.'

'I don't know who Geoffrey Pinkleton is. Sorry.' She started to close the door, but Jim persisted.

'Geoffrey Pinkleton is your son. And he needs your help.'

Angela suddenly looked as though she had seen a ghost. She reluctantly opened the door

'You'd best come in...'

Geoffrey sat on the mattress in his prison cell, contemplating the situation that he now found himself in. It didn't look good. DNA was the lifeblood of convictions for the police; once they had that it would be an invitation to lock him up and throw away the key. How was that possible? Poor Olivia, he thought, what must she be going through? It's not fair. Everything that had happened was beyond his control. For the first time in his life, Geoffrey felt helpless and totally alone.

Jim sat on an armchair by a small coffee table while Angela stood nearby and poured tea from a teapot into two cups. She then sat opposite him.

'How did you find me?' asked Angela.

'I'm a probate researcher,' said Jim, 'We specialise in genealogy. I checked the General Register Office. It has records of births deaths and adoptions. I then spoke with Geoff's parents who confirmed that they had adopted him when he was a baby. I contacted the adoption agency. It's part of my job to find out long-lost relations. I also have access to records most people aren't even aware of. If you want to remain anonymous, I will fully understand and respect your decision.'

Angela smiled and nodded. 'Too much water under the bridge…'

There was a poignant lull in the conversation.

'What can you tell me about your circumstances – what made you put Geoffrey up for adoption?'

Angela had a sad expression in her eyes. It was as if a memory that she had suppressed for so long had suddenly come back to haunt her once more.

'I was fifteen. So young… I was raped… He was a friend of the family. My parents trusted him. I trusted him… How wrong can you be?' Angela wiped away a tear with a handkerchief. 'You said Geoffrey was in trouble?'

Jim nodded. 'He's in prison awaiting a trial for something that he didn't do.'

'How can you be so sure?'

'He wouldn't hurt a fly. But his DNA was at the scene of the crime.'

'So? How can I possibly help?'

'You see, his fingerprints didn't match.'

'I don't understand?'

Jim leant in close to Angela. 'You had identical twins. Isn't that right?'

Tears suddenly streamed down Angela's cheeks as the realisation of Jim's statement made its impact...

Jim sat in his car, mulling over the information that he had gathered from Geoffrey's real mother. He made a phone call from his mobile phone. 'DI Jennings please. It's urgent.'

It took a long time for Jennings to answer.

'DI Jennings. How can I help you?'

Four days passed. Jim visited Geoffrey in prison to tell him of his findings. They sat opposite each other at a small table in the visiting room under the careful watch of prison officers.

'I have a twin brother?' Geoffrey was in total shock. It took a long time for the information to sink in.

'Your real mother, who asks to be left alone, said she and her parents felt that her sons would have a better chance of being adopted if they were separated. You were taken up by an adoption agency, while your brother was passed to a distant relation as one of their own.'

'I always knew I was adopted, but had no idea I had a brother. I've always felt that a part of me was missing – now it makes perfect sense.'

'It explains why your DNA was found at the scene of the crime; you see, identical twins have the same DNA.'

'If his fingerprints match those on the assault weapon then it's an open and shut case... And you've told the police all of this?'

Jim nodded. 'They're out there now. It's just a matter of time.'

Geoffrey had mixed feelings and a hundred and one questions that he wanted to ask, but where to start? 'What's his name?'

'Anthony. Anthony Grainger.'

'Grainger? That's the same name as the old man who was assaulted…'

Later that evening a sheepish DI Jennings entered Geoffrey's cell, accompanied by DI Simms. 'I'm pleased to say that you're free to go, Mister Pinkleton. We've now arrested the real perpetrator.' As an afterthought, he added, 'Thanks to your friend's information.'

'And you're sure this time? You won't be knocking on our door in the early hours of the morning?'

Jennings shook his head. 'Anthony Grainger's fingerprints were matched to those on the assault weapon. He's given us a full confession. I take it you didn't know you had a twin brother?'

'It's not the best way to find out, is it? Where is he?'

'He's actually in the cell next to yours.'

Geoffrey's curiosity was piqued. 'Can I see him? Just for a short while?'

Jennings thought it over. 'It's not normal procedure, but what with all you've had to go through I'm sure we can allow you a few minutes alone with your brother.'

Geoffrey was taken to the next cell. When the door was opened, the sight of his twin brother sitting on his mattress took his breath away. It was like looking in a mirror. Even their hairstyle was the same.

Anthony stood and faced his newly-found twin brother. 'Good god. I had no idea you even existed.'

'Me neither.'

Anthony went to shake Geoffrey's hand but Geoffrey declined.

'What you did was so wrong,' said Geoffrey.

Anthony looked ashamed. 'I realise that now, but that bastard made my life hell. You have no idea what I went through as a kid being raised by that psycho.'

Geoffrey suddenly felt deep empathy for his brother. 'I'm so sorry. I had no idea.'

'He had a temper. Made my life hell. And that wasn't the half of it. I'll spare you the details… Even now I'm not able to sleep properly.'

'I'm sure the courts will take all that into consideration.' Geoffrey offered his hand, and Anthony shook it gladly. 'We'll stay in touch. Make up for lost time. I'll get you a good lawyer.'

They embraced.

Geoffrey was taken by police car back to his home. On the journey, Geoffrey thought over past events in his head. It had been a strange traumatic experience. What his brother did was wrong, he considered, but it sounded as though the old man had ruined his life. Poor Anthony. Life can be so cruel. He then appreciated, ironically, just how good *he* had it. He had a loving partner and a wonderful home life. He was lucky…

Olivia, dog in hand, greeted Geoffrey as he opened the front door. They fell into each other's arms and kissed tenderly. Trace tried his best to get in on the action and licked Geoffrey for all he was worth.

'Let's go to bed,' announced Olivia, overjoyed.

'You took the words right out of my mouth,' replied an exhausted Geoffrey.

They closed the door.

Colin Fantham BA (hons)
Colin Fantham was born in Stratford-upon-Avon in 1957. Having spent over 40 years in the insurance industry he is now retired and devotes most of his energy to his writing. Creative from an early age, Colin has written several pieces of music and numerous scripts for stage and screen.
Some examples of his work:

Henry's Last Act. A half hour original comedy series for television. It is set in The Sunny Retreat retirement home for entertainers. This gentle comedy centres around the friendship between residents Henry, Edgar and Twinky, as well as an abundance of other quirky characters, including Jessica who is a teenage work-experience employee. 8 episodes. PublishNation in Amazon.

Henry's Last Act
Sitcom for TV - 8 episodes
Colin Fantham

The Folly (A Moment in Time). A 5 act stage play. A late Victorian period drama involving 2 families (The Hathertons and the Buckleys) who happen to meet by a folly. Their chance encounter leads to a path of destruction, love, but ultimately self-enlightenment. Is the enchanted area of the folly a reality, or from the mind of a

man on the brink of despair? Atmospheric and magical. PublishNation in Amazon.

Visitors from a Lost World. A 2 act stage play. Arthur, who is an elderly gentleman, lives alone in a remote tower block in London with only his fish Merlin for company. He narrates his past to Merlin, and we see him in his youth when he served his national service in the 1950s and fell in love with Dotty. Funny, sad, and poignant. PublishNation in Amazon.

The Final Chapter of A Strange Affair. A 2 act stage play. In 1969, Peter is a writer on the edge of madness. Suffering from writer's block, he is unable to meet the deadline for submission of his latest novel A Strange Affair. All is not as it seems, as Peter is still troubled by the mysterious disappearance of his wife Angela. A chilling insight into the mind of a writer who is haunted by events of the past. And then there's George... Dark and frightening. PublishNation in Amazon.

A compilation of three plays: The Folly (A Moment In Time); Visitors from a Lost World; The Final Chapter of A Strange Affair. PublishNation in Amazon.

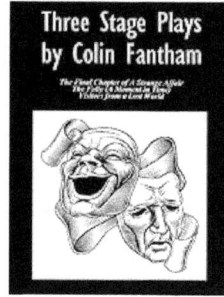

A film script based on the play Visitors from a Lost World. PublishNation in Amazon.

In Search of The Lost Galaxy is a 2 act stage play. An old man, worried that he is losing his mind, seeks the help of a psychiatrist to analyse the mysterious dreams that he's been having. As each dream is relayed by the old man, a disturbing story unfolds. The lines of fantasy and reality become blurred, but remain inexplicably linked. A heartbreaking journey of discovery that will resonate with many family members. PublishNation in Amazon.

Copyright © All rights reserved

www.ingramcontent.com/pod-product-compliance
Ingram Content Group UK Ltd.
Pitfield, Milton Keynes, MK11 3LW, UK
UKHW020612311025
8692UKWH00006B/267